Money Mafia 2

Lock Down Publications and Ca$h
Presents

Money Mafia 2

A Novel by *Jibril Williams*

Lock Down Publications
P.O. Box 944
Stockbridge, Ga 30281
www.lockdownpublications.com

Lock Down Publications
Like our page on Facebook: Lock Down Publications @
www.facebook.com/lockdownpublications.ldp

Book interior design by: **Shawn Walker**
Edited by: **Mia Rucker**

Stay Connected with Us!

Text **LOCKDOWN** to 22828 to stay up-to-date with new releases, sneak peaks, contests and more...

Thank you!

Submission Guideline.

Submit the first three chapters of your completed manuscript to ldpsubmissions@gmail.com, subject line: Your book's title. The manuscript must be in a .doc file and sent as an attachment. Document should be in Times New Roman, double spaced and in size 12 font. Also, provide your synopsis and full contact information. If sending multiple submissions, they must each be in a separate email.

Have a story but no way to send it electronically? You can still submit to LDP/Ca$h Presents. Send in the first three chapters, written or typed, of your completed manuscript to:

LDP: Submissions Dept
P.O. Box 944
Stockbridge, Ga 30281

DO NOT send original manuscript. Must be a duplicate.

Provide your synopsis and a cover letter containing your full contact information.

Thanks for considering LDP and Ca$h Presents.

Chapter 1

"I think it's about time we merge the two families together. Money Mafia and Oxon Hill Mafia Boyz should be under the same umbrella. The merging of the two families will triple the profits. Also, it will show our growth and strength." Brim paused and stared into the eyes of everyone that occupied the backroom of Ace Electronics.

Jus-Blaze stared at Brim like he was the dumbest nigga ever, hearing the statement come out Brim's mouth had him wanting to voice his opinion about the matter. He had animosity towards members of Oxon Hill Mafia Boyz for stomping him out inside the Stadium Strip Club on Musa's birthday. Jus-Blaze felt he didn't get a chance to get his payback on Oxon Hill Mafia Boyz. The only reason he hadn't paid the Oxon Hill Mafia back yet was because Musa went to prison on a parole violation, and Brim took leadership over Money Mafia and had ordered him to put the beef on hold until Money Mafia could recover from losing Musa, Ace and Shoota. But now Brim was trying to bring both families together, and that wasn't sitting right with Jus-Blaze.

"I'm trying to take Money Mafia to the next level. My vision of taking us to the next level and doing things on a level of sophistication will only work by combining the organizations."

Stink sat at the round table with his hands steepled together in front of him and his elbows rested on the Oakwood table. Sharkhead sat next to him, and he was respecting every word that was coming out of Brim's mouth. Ever since Musa took the minor setback, Brim was in charge and Stink and Sharkhead were more than satisfied with the new leadership. With Brim being in charge, he gave them more power and responsibilities than they normally would have under Musa's leadership. With Musa gone, it allowed them to have unlimited access to the trap houses and all money went through their hands, before it touched Brim's.

Sharkhead was one of those dudes that got his name based on his physical appearance. Sharkhead had a mouth full of teeth that seemed to overlap one another, like a shark. And he had the aggressive attitude of the ocean apex predator. Sharkhead was built, with a clean-shaved head. Sharkhead stood 5'8" with the skin tone of black oil. He struggled badly with power orientation, manipulation, intimidation, and physically assaulting others was Sharkhead's way of life. When Musa was in charge, he kept Sharkhead's power orientation issues in check. But with Brim running things, Sharkhead conducted himself in any manner he saw fit, and Brim said nothing, as long as the money kept coming in.

"Aye, Slim, I got a suggestion, since we discussing coming together and shit, under one conformity. Since you the head of Money Mafia and I'm the head of Oxon Hill Mafia Boyz, it's only right that I take seat at second command," Pop-Roc announced from his chair. He watched Brim's body language like a guard dog would watch a trespasser, right before he would launch his attack. Brim was aware that Stink, Jus-Blaze, and Sharkhead had eyes on him, right along with Pop-Roc's inner circle of Oxon Hill Mafia. Brim picked the bottle of Henny up off the table and refilled his empty glass. He lifted the glass.

"If the merge goes well, I appoint you as second in command," Brim said, downing the drink.

Pop-Roc smiled but he had another question. "What about Musa? What position would Musa play in all of this? How would Musa feel about all of this? Before he left, he was totally against Money Mafia doing any kind of business with us. So I know that he's gonna speak out against the merge."

8

Brim sat there and contemplated Pop-Roc's question before he answered. "How could Musa be against something that no longer concerns him? Musa no longer has a stake in Money Mafia. The Mafia belongs to me. The Mafia will be dictated under our leadership." Brim spoke with wickedness in his voice.

Jus-Blaze was ready to jump out of his chair and protest the bullshit that Brim's young ass was preaching, but Stink kicked his foot, warning him to fall back. Pop-Roc shook his head up and down in agreement. If Brim was really about what he was preaching, then he knew he was definitely getting ready to see some real money. The only thing that stopped Oxon Hill Mafia from elevating to Money Mafia's level was the fact that they didn't have a constant supplier. They were hitting and missing when it came to product.

Pop-Roc stood to his feet and walked over to Brim, and the two embraced. The embrace sealed the deal on the merge. "We getting ready to see a lot of money, Pop. I hope that you have them counting machines on standby because you gonna need them."

***

The courtroom was extremely silent when Ace walked in the Maryland Superior Courtroom. The only thing that could be heard was the jiggle of the shackles and belly chain that secured her ankles and wrists with every shift and shuffle she made to get into the courtroom. The more she moved with the slave jewelry she had on, the louder the chain jiggled.

Ace looked through the sea of reporters and she found a familiar face in the mix of them. Mama Cheryl stared at her with loving eyes. She tilted her chin up in the air signaling for Ace to be strong, and Ace acknowledged the gesture with a head nod. She held her head high as she took her place next to her attorney, Ashley Stoner. Mama Cheryl had been loyal to the soil throughout Ace's situation, even before Ace was charged with murder for killing Musa's parole officer. Mama Cheryl had been nothing but a mother figure to Ace. Mama Cheryl was the reason why she had the top-notch attorney, Ms. Ashley Stoner. Once Ace was arrested for murder, she reached out to Mama Cheryl, giving her the combination to her personal safe. She instructed Mama Cheryl to remove her money and hire her an attorney to assist her in fighting for her freedom, and Mama Cheryl came through for Ace.

Ashley Stoner was the best lawyer that the State of Maryland had ever produced. Her rap sheet as a lawyer was impeccable. She specialized in defending defendants in murder and capital punishment cases. Through her seventeen years as a lawyer, Ms. Stoner never lost a murder case. Ms. Stoner defended 39 clients for the crime of murder, and all were home in the comfort of their homes. But the case and client she was representing today had her uncertain she could remain undefeated in the courtroom.

"Dana Foster, here on behalf of the government, Your Honor," the prosecutor addressed the courts, putting Ace's hearing in motion.

"Ashley Stoner, here on behalf of my client, Ace Altidort."

The Honorable Henderson looked down from his bench at Ace. His stare was cold. And there wasn't a hint of caring in his eyes. "I'm Judge James Henderson, and I will be seeing the function of this case. Ace Altidort v. The State of Maryland," Judge Henderson said, leaning back in his chair and giving his attention to the prosecutor, Mr. Foster. And like a trained dog, Mr. Foster went right into action.

"Your Honor, Ms. Altidort is charged with first degree murder, attempted murder, attempted murder of a child, and child endangerment. We ask that Ms. Altidort remain in custody, without bail, pending her trial date."

Hearing all the charges she was being accused of put a tightness in her chest. The healing gunshot wounds didn't make it easier for her to breathe. Ace started to feel lightheaded.

"Your Honor, there is no need to hold Ms. Altidort without a bail. She is not a flight risk, nor is she a threat to the public. Ms. Altidort should be given a bond and at least released on the ankle monitor. My client is recovering from two gunshot wounds to her chest. A county jail is no place for my client to be trying to recover from such injuries." Ms. Stoner moved some papers around on the cherry oakwood desk that she stood in front of. "Your Honor, Ms. Altidort is a member of the community. She's the proud owner of Ace Electronics. She employs 22 employees-"

Mr. Foster cut Ms. Stoner off. "Your Honor, Ms. Altidort is much of a flight risk. The government has information that Ms. Altidort has strong ties to the street gang, Money Mafia. It has also been brought to our attention that Ms. Altidort killed the parole officer of Money Mafia's leader for violating his parole."

Upon hearing this, Ace's chest became tighter and even though the air conditioner in the courtroom was on full blast, she was still able to break out in sweat.

"Your Honor," Ms. Stoner butted in. "There's no proof that my client is even affiliated with the gang Money Mafia or that she even knew the gang leader or murdered his parole officer and attempted to murder his family," Ms. Stoner said firmly.

Mr. Foster went for the neck. "Your Honor, the government asks that the court deny bail for Ms. Altidort simply because we are seeking the death penalty in this matter."

When Ace heard the words "death penalty," her knees buckled, and Ms. Stoner tried to catch her before she fell to the courtroom floor, but it was too late. Ace blacked out.

Chapter 2

The lines across Musa's forehead creased, a confused look fell upon his face. The news his father, Moses, just conveyed to him had him wanting to fight. He flexed the muscles in his jaw and fought to compose the rage that was brewing inside of him. The city of DC wasn't but so big, and there was only one Ace that roamed the city, and that was Ace, his partner, his Queen Money Mafia second in command.

"Come on, pops, you're not gonna stand in my face, after all these years you have been missing in my life, and tell me that Ace is my fucking sister!" Musa raised his voice, drawing some attention from some of the inmates on the prison yard.

Moses stepped into Musa's personal space.

"Lower your voice!" Moses said through clenched teeth.

Moses was an OG. He hated for attention to be brought to him. Musa could smell the morning coffee on his father's breath. The man wasn't that brute of a man that Musa remembered him to be. Cancer had taken a toll of his clad body, but that fire still resided in his eyes. Musa took half a step back.

"Now I know that you don't want to hear that Ace is your sister, but the situation is what it is, just another hard pill for you to swallow. But that's life, son."

"A hard pill to swallow? We talking more like a fucking brick that I'm trying to swallow. Do you know the fucking damage you have caused by not letting me know that Ace is my sister? Do you know all the dysfunctional shit you created in our lives by you not sitting us down and telling us that we were related, letting us know we shared the same bloodline? Pops, you foul as fuck for that!" Musa yammered.

"Son, I know shit seems fucked up and you have every right to feel the way you feel. But the facts are what they are, and neither one of us can change them facts. That's why when

I heard that you and Ace was out there hustling in the streets together, I reached out to you. Somehow you two found each other in the dark. It was ordained for you to be in each other's lives."

"No, pops, shit deeper than that! Ace is my Queen. She's my rib, the rhythm of my heartbeat."

Now it was Moses's turn for the lines in his forehead to crease. "What you saying, Musa, you fucking your sister?" Now Moses understood the depth of his anger. He felt like shit just from the thought of his two children having sexual relations with one another.

"No, pops, we haven't fucked, but we came so fucking close! And I mean we came so close, pops. But my intuition always screamed at me when we came close to having sex," Musa said.

He couldn't even believe that he was having this type of conversation with his father.

"Well, it's a good thing that you never became intimate with your sister. Now you won't have a problem putting you and your sister's relationship in the proper perspective."

"What the fuck you don't understand, pops? My love for Ace runs deeper than a sister. I'm in love with her, pops. I just can't turn that shit off like a light switch."

"Musa, if you can't turn that shit off like a light switch, then you need to knock the light bulb out that bitch, because no son of mine is fucking with his sister." Moses stepped in his son's personal space for the second time. This time Musa didn't take a step back.

"Pops, I don't give a fuck what you say. I'm gonna love Ace the way that I always been loving her," Musa stated through clenched teeth.

His father searched his son's eyes for seriousness, and he saw nothing but conviction in them. That troubled him. He had to figure out another way to break the son and daughter relationship up. He had to take a different approach. Musa was too much like him. He was stubborn, when he had his mind and heart set on something. Moses took a step back from Musa. He could see that a group of inmates on the yard noticed their heated exchange.

"Musa, I need to speak with Ace. Can you please give me her number?"

For the first time, it dawned on Musa that his father didn't know what had transpired with Ace. He immediately put his head down. His eyes glazed with tears. The thought of Ace being arrested for murder tore at his heart.

"Dad, I have to tell you something about Ace."

All the years that Musa had been his son, he had never known his son to cry. Whatever it was about Ace, it must be a grave matter.

"What's going on with my baby girl, Musa? What's up with your sister?" Moses asked with concern in his voice.

Musa let out a deep breath. "She, she killed my parole officer for violating my parole. She's sitting in county jail awaiting trial," Musa lifted his head and faced his father.

Moses put his arm around Musa's neck and guided him towards the track. "Tell me everything, Musa. I want to know every detail."

***

Ace blacking out in court was perceived as nothing. They rushed her back to county jail and had a nurse look at her. She was given some oxygen and some water and sent her back to her unit. Walking back to her cell, she unfolded the court papers she held in her hand. Scanning over the papers made her feel a bit of lassitude. She initially wanted to call Musa to share the bad news she got from court. But before she could muster up the strength to call Musa, she walked in the cell where she found Tammy's head buried in a book called "Friend or Foe" by Mimi.

Tammy heard her cell door open. She removed the book from her face to see who just walked into the cell, disturbing her reading time. She saw it was Ace. The walking dead look Ace had plastered across her face made her dogear the page she was reading to find out what was going on with her celly.

Ace had been nothing but a real friend to Tammy since she had met her. Tammy kept the wolves out of Ace's ass until she healed up from her bullet wounds. When Ace first came in the unit, she was in bad shape. Tammy took care of her and nursed her back to health. Tammy climbed down from her bunk, placing her feet in a pair of orange shower slides.

"Ace, baby, what's wrong? Are you okay?" Tammy asked, her voice laced with concern.

Ace replied by handing Tammy her court papers and dropping down to her knees, crying. Tammy scanned the motion quickly and started to cry when she read the State of Maryland was seeking the death penalty if Ace was convicted.

Chapter 3

Musa had told his pops everything leading up to Ace killing his parole officer. He even told his pops about the dilemma he was in with Shoota and how Shoota wanted him to kill Papaya because he thought Musa allowed Papaya to green light him to get shot. They both came up with all kinds of scenarios on how to handle Musa's situation. There was no way Musa would ever walk out of prison a free man if he killed Papaya inside Wackin Hunt prison. This could never be done without a sacrifice.

Moses was crushed to learn that his daughter was sitting in a county jail. Musa told his father he would set it up for him to talk to Ace if she wanted to talk to him.

Musa got up from his bunk. He took a leak and washed his hands. "Ace is your sister." Them words kept ringing through his head.

Musa checked the G-Shock watch. It was 3:30 P.M. He had 30 minutes before the prison conducted their four o'clock count. He was going to wait until they counted before he brought his phone out. He needed to call his mother. He needed to talk with her. He had so many things on his mind. He wanted to get his mother's input on Ace being his sister and plus, he wanted to find out what had happened at Ace's court date today.

A tap came to Musa's door. It was the Unit Secretary. Ms. Lacey waved Musa out of the cell. Ms. Lacey was a thick, cornbread fed, brown-skinned woman, with a shapely figure. Ms. Lacey was beautiful, but she was old enough to be Musa's mother. But that didn't stop him from checking her out from time to time, whenever she made her presence known in the unit.

"Mr. Blackwell, you have legal mail." Ms. Lacey started smiling. She handed Musa the logbook, where she had him sign for the certified mail.

Ms. Lacey stuck to the institution's process on inmates receiving legal mail. She opened the mail in front of Musa and inspected it for contraband, before handing Musa his mail. The whole time Ms. Lacey was inspecting his mail, Musa was checking her full lips out.

"I hope it's some good news. You too handsome to be in here with these animals," Ms. Lacey whispered, giving Musa her award-winning smile, and walked away.

Musa wanted to stand there and watch Ms. Lacey walk because doing so was a show to watch, but he quickly realized that he had eyes on him and Ms. Lacey. That was one thing in prison, someone always had a set of eyes on you.

Musa stepped back into his cell and placed the flap up over his window for some privacy. He took a seat on his bunk and looked at the front of the envelope. It was addressed from the D.C. Parole Commissioner.

Musa had been sitting in prison over the last four months on a three-year violation. Musa's parole officer had him violated when he learned that Musa had his only brother, One-Punch, murdered. What had Musa madder than strippers without a pole to perform on was the fact Brim had orchestrated the whole play for the parole officer, Mr. Braxton, to violate him. Brim turned out to be One-Punch's son. This was a revelation that Musa knew nothing about. If he did, he would have never allowed Brim to kill his own dad. Out of loyalty and love for Musa, Ace jumped the gun and murdered the parole officer for his transgression.

Musa was baffled how one small drop of a pebble in the pond could create so many ripples in his water. Musa wondered what the Parole Commissioner would have to say to him. The Commissioner already contacted him and notified him that his violation was confirmed and his appeal was denied. But for some reason, when Musa unfolded the letter, his hands became sweaty and they shook. He began to read the letter wrong. But once he finished, he came up with the same conclusion.

The letter stated that through an investigation, it was determined that parole officer Mr. Braxton was corrupt and took money from other parolees in hope of not violating them. The parole commissioner apologized for Mr. Braxton's conduct and ensured Musa that his parole would be reinstated within the next ninety days of receiving his letter.

***

"You niggas crazy as fuck to even consider going along with this shit Brim trying to pull. This nigga talking about cutting the big homie out the picture, and joining forces with Pop-Roc and them." Jus-Blaze rolled a phat Backwood, while he complained to Sharkhead and Stink.

"What the fuck you want us to do, Slim? Fuck the money train up, because we supposed to be loyal to Musa?" Stink stated.

"Naw, you niggas loyal to Musa. I'm loyal to whoever keep me eating, and right now, them blue notes is what's keeping the roof over my kid's head and wifey laced in that drip and draped in nothing but designers," Sharkhead said, cutting Stink off. He poured himself a shot of Henny. He was getting irritated with Jus-Blaze because he'd been complaining about the merge with Oxon Hill Mafia and the fact Brim said fuck Musa.

"It's loyalty over money, it's not money over loyalty. You niggas got your principles wrong. Real Money Mafia members don't operate under false principles. That's for them fake niggas," Jus-Blaze yammered with his face balled up. Sharkhead had him hot.

"Nigga, your soft ass questioning my G? You calling me out, Slim?" Shark raised his voice.

"Slim, I'm not checking your G. All I'm saying is you need to check your own G because you talking like a well put together sucka."

"Jus-Blaze, you better watch your mouth before you find yourself misplaced, with your head in your lap," Sharkhead said smoothly.

"Nigga, that shit goes both ways, Slim, the last time I checked," Jus-Blaze announced without an ounce of fear in his voice.

"Come on, you niggas tripping. Jus, I understood where your heart at when it comes to Musa. But at the end of the day, Musa gonna be gone for the next three years. You going hard for Musa, but if you stop and get your head out Musa's ass, Musa didn't leave you with nothing, he left it with Brim. And if Brim saying fuck 'em, then I advise you do the same before Brim says fuck you. You know what happens then. Them Goons coming and they ain't talking, Slim. So, get this money while we can. Every well runs dry sooner or later."

Stink just gave it to him blood raw, but still shit didn't sit right with him. He just had to see where the movement took him. He wished that Shoota was there. There was no question that Shoota would've had shit running smoothly, and there would be no talk of merging with Pop-Roc.

"You know what, you dead ass right, and I'm dead ass wrong. Nigga under a lot of stress." Jus-Blaze stood to his feet and shook it up with Stink. When he extended his hand to Sharkhead, it was met with hesitation. Sharkhead was about to say something slick until his baby's moms, Nay, walked in the living room, looking like a new stripper in a pair of boy shorts and tank top, with her 11-month-old riding her hip. When Sharkhead saw what she had on, the smart remark he had for Jus-Blaze disappeared as he snapped on Nay and told her to put some fucking clothes on. Jus-Blaze made his way out of Sharkhead's apartment with a smirk on his face.

Chapter 4

Brim sat behind the wheel of his 2021 Range Rover sport, as he floated the vehicle through Pennsylvania Ave N.W. He was heading back to Ledorit Park Projects, nodding his head to the DC Native, Wale, featuring Jammie Foxx, "Dearly Beloved." The boy, Wale, was on his grown man shit. Brim was feeling the track because he, too, was on his grown man shit. These last few months were a blur. He went from getting money to being money. It was a whole different level he was on.

As Wale rapped his verse, Brim rapped the verse to Cynthia, who sat on the passenger side of the Range, looking like a sexy Nikki Minaj, just an older version, though. Cynthia smiled at Brim, even though she didn't think the lyrics of the song fit her and Brim's situation. She was just happy that Brim was showing her some attention.

"Dearly Beloved, I was lucky to love ya but I ain't recovered yet." Brim rapped, flicking his finger across Cynthia's nipple, which was pressing against her Chanel blouse. The nipple grew harder under Brim's touch.

"Thank you for taking me to the Black History Museum. That was very nice of you."

"You know it's all good. You been asking me to go for a while, so I had to do that for you," Brim's young ass said with smoothness, navigating the truck onto Florida Avenue.

Even though Cynthia grew up in the heart of DC and was about thirteen years older than Brim, she loved two things, Black History and Brim. She'd never met a young man that treated her so royally. There wasn't anything she wouldn't do for Brim, and there wasn't anything that Brim wouldn't do for her. But she was having problems with him being the head nigga in charge of Money Mafia. She didn't see him as often as she used to when he worked under Musa. Now that he was running the Mafia, she had to fight him tooth and nails just to spend some time with him.

"So, you coming to see me later?"

Brim sped the truck up, once he made it to 1st Street. He wanted to get Cynthia out of his truck as quickly as he could. He made a right into LeDroit Park Projects and stopped the truck in front of the building.

"Sorry, bae, a nigga got so much shit to do." Brim finally answered Cynthia's question.

"Nope, that ain't what a bitch trying to hear. I need to see you tonight, Brim," Cynthia pouted.

"Cyn, I got moves and money to make," Brim capped, turning the music down in the truck and checking his mirrors. Some of the workers in the projects watched Brim's truck. They knew it was him sitting in the white Range with the black 28-inch rims. The tints sat dark on the truck, which made it hard for his workers to see him.

Cynthia unbuckled her seatbelt and turned sideways in her seat. She reached over and grabbed Brim's dick through his Louie Vuitton jeans. The aggressive sexual nature always got Brim worked up.

"When I'ma see you?" Cynthia asked again.

"Stop playing. I told you I got a bunch of shit to handle. You know the grind never stops," Brim confessed.

Cynthia slowly stroked Brim through his jeans, until she felt him stiffen. "That's not an answer, Brim, and it's sure not a response I wanted to hear." Cynthia unbuckled Brim's jeans and freed his meat bat.

Once the smoothness and softness of her hand touched the bare skin on Brim's dick, it was a new sensation for Brim and his pipe swelled under the contact.

"So when will I see you?" Cynthia asked again.

Brim let out a deep breath. At that moment, he was a fiend and Cynthia was his fix.

"Bae, stop playing, a nigga gotta be somewhere."

Brim tried to remove Cynthia's hand. She quickly slapped his hand away from hers. She let the saliva build up in her mouth. She leaned over and allowed a glob of spit to drop out of her mouth onto Brim's dick. She worked her hand in an up and down motion, using her spit as a lubricant on Brim's dick. She took her thumb and used it to run track around the head of Brim's pipe.

"Shit, Cynthia, put the dick in your mouth," Brim moaned.

Cynthia leaned over and kissed Brim roughly. He loved that aggressive shit. He palmed the back of Cynthia's head and fed her tongue. He had his tongue so deep in Cyn's mouth, he felt her tonsils. Cynthia removed her lips from Brim's. They both were breathing hard. She went down on Brim, slurping his pipe to the back of her throat. She then placed Brim's hand on the back of her head and went into superhead mode.

Cynthia was eating Brim's dick, like she was born for that purpose only. She located a perfect pace and hummed on the dick, while she went up and down on it. Brim squeezed his eyes tightly and opened them in time to catch Cynthia watching him. Cynthia had beautiful, bubble eyes that made a man cum in two point two seconds, if he looked into her eyes while she had his dick in her mouth. And that's what was about to happen. Cynthia could feel Brim about to cum in her mouth and she abruptly stopped. She opened the truck's door and got out.

"What the fuck you doing? Cyn, get the fuck back on this dick," Brim said, looking at Cyn like he could beat her ass right then and there.

He was breathing hard, dick sticking straight up and glazed over from Cynthia's saliva.

"What time you coming through later?" Cynthia asked, straightening out her Chanel blouse.

"Slim, I'm gonna get you back for this, Cyn," Brim stated.

"That's cool, just come through tonight and you can pay me back." Cyn blew him a kiss and closed the truck's door.

Cynthia walked towards her building. Even though Brim was mad as hell for the stunt Cyn just pulled, he still admired her ass. Cyn turned around and smiled because she knew Brim was watching her. So, she added a little extra swing to her hips, hoping she had enough bounce in her ass to bring Brim to her bed tonight.

Brim tucked his piece in his jeans and pulled away from Cynthia's building. He didn't even holla at the niggas in the projects. He remembered how he used to hang on them same corners and hustle off them same project buildings. He felt like stopping and hollering at the corner workers was beneath him. even though these were the same muthafuckas that pushed his product. He would let Sharkhead and them deal with the corner level dealers. His concern was finding a plug that was strong enough to supply him and the merge. He was tired of fucking with Musa. He wanted his independence. Even while Musa was in prison, he was still in Musa's shadow. And that wasn't something he could continue to do much longer.

Brim's mind turned to Shoota. He still couldn't put the piece together on what really happened. He was guessing that Ace killed Shoota after catching him and her girlfriend, Jassii, together. That was the only reason why Jassii ended up dead in Shoota's truck. Through news reports, it was mentioned that Shoota's blood was all over the driver's seat of the truck. There was no doubt that Shoota was hurt badly, but where was his body at? Ace must have kidnapped him after she shot him and Jassii. She must have taken Shoota somewhere and buried him. Nevertheless, though, he wished Shoota was there to see his success.

Brim's thoughts turned to Ace. He hated that bitch with his last breath. "She had no place in this man's game," Brim thought to himself. The night he found out that Musa's PO was his uncle, he knew that he had to kill her. He just wished he would have dome checked her, instead of shooting her in the chest twice.

Brim pulled up at Sussex Square Apartments. This was the third time he had been there since Musa went to prison. He checked the surroundings before getting out of his truck. He made his way to the building quickly and quietly. He stood in front of the door and listened intensely before he knocked. He knocked several times, but no one came to the door. For a second, he thought he saw the peephole on the door darken, but he was quickly distracted by one of the building's residents leaving their apartment. The heavy-set white chick smile at Brim and kept it moving. Brim wanted to ask her if she knew Mama Cheryl, but he refused to ask because he didn't want to bring attention to himself. So, he just left and made a note to slide back through another time.

Jibril Williams

28

Chapter 5

Mama Cheryl made it home safely from Ace's court hearing. The dramatic court hearing left her with an upset stomach and a killer migraine. Her head was hurting her so badly that she could feel a pulse in it. She came home and immediately laid across her bed, without even cutting the TV or radio on. She needed pure silence to overcome her headaches.

The migraine and the words "death penalty" wouldn't allow her to rest. So, she laid across her Queen-size bed in prayer, asking the good lord to remove her headache, and make her hardship easy. The whole ordeal, with the prosecutor asking for the death penalty and Ace fainting, broke her heart. She laid in bed forty-five minutes with her eyes close to crying. She loved Ace, and no matter what she had done, Ace doesn't deserve a death sentence. Ace was like a daughter to her. Despite Musa being stubborn, Ace would make a great daughter-in-law, if Musa would even give Ace a chance at his heart.

Mama Cheryl wondered how Ace was doing and if she was able to get some medical attention. She wondered about her own son. Musa was sitting in prison for a parole violation. She didn't know how she was going to make it, without Musa, for the next three years. With the money Musa had left her to manage and with Ace's stash of money, she would be well off long after Musa came home. But every day Musa was away, a part of her was dying. She missed her son dearly.

Mama Cheryl opened an eye and examined the time on her watch. Her headache was starting to subside, but the bubbling of her stomach became worse. She broke wind and instantly could smell the foul odor that escaped from inside of her. She crinkled up her nose and buried her face into the pillow to avoid her body gases.

"God damn, Cheryl, you smell like a full-grown man," she spoke into the pillow.

A sharp pain hit her stomach again. She felt the need to sit on the toilet, but she wanted to wait until Ace or Musa called before she did that. She didn't want to miss either of their calls.

Knock. Knock. Knock.

A knock came to Mama Cheryl's apartment door. She just laid there for a minute, hoping whoever it was would go away. She wasn't in the mood to be hosting company. So, she closed her eyes tighter and wished the pain in her stomach to go away. But whoever it was wasn't going away, because they let their knuckles tap on her door again.

She let out a deep breath and forced herself out of bed. She staggered towards the door, halfway bent over, with a hand over her stomach. She really didn't have the strength to yell out, "Who is it?" She wondered who was at her door as she made her way to see who the person was with the bad timing.

She placed a hand on the doorknob, got on her tip toes, and peeped through the peephole. Who she saw on the other side of the door made her retreat like a group of Jehovah's Witnesses was on the other side of it. Her headache and upset stomach were instantly gone. Brim was at her door. She wondered if he saw her shadow through the peephole. He was turning his head as her neighbor was coming out of her apartment.

Mama Cheryl's heart thumped hard in her chest, shortening her breath. She scurried away from the door, moving quickly towards her bedroom. With quivering hands, Mama Cheryl retrieved her phone from the bed, and in one quick motion she was pulling her 38 special from between her mattress. Mama Cheryl had lived a hard life as a drug addict. One thing the streets taught her was defense. If you didn't learn that number one rule of survival, you would, without question, become a victim of your environment. She cocked the hammer back on her 38 and advanced towards the front of the apartment.

Ace had already warned her that Brim wasn't to be trusted, through decoded conversation. Mama Cheryl had learned that Brim was the one that had shot Ace. She was on the phone when Brim tried to take Ace's life. This was the third time Brim had come past her apartment, unannounced, to pay her a visit. Since it had been deemed that he was the weak and deadly link in the chain, she wasn't taking any chances with being in the presence of Brim by herself. So, when Brim came past, she played possum, and acted like she wasn't home.

Going back to her door, she peeked out the peephole and Brim was gone. She immediately went to the living room window and peered out the crack of the curtain. She was just in time to see Brim getting in his truck. She took a deep breath and uncocked her 38. She let the weapon hang at her side in her hand.

"Bitch nigga, what do you want? Why you keep coming past my place?" Mama Cheryl mumbled to herself. And just that quickly, the bubbling sensation was back in her stomach. She made a beeline to the bathroom, dropped her pants and panties, and sat on the toilet.

Mama Cheryl rested the gun on the shoulder of the tub and emptied out her bowels. Instantly, she was granted relief.

The phone in her hand started vibrating. It was Musa calling. Mama Cheryl hit the talk icon and put the phone on speaker.

"Hello."

"Wassup, Ma," Musa said. He didn't know if he should start the conversation with the news of Ace being his father's daughter or the news that he would be gaining his freedom back in the next few months.

"Oh, hey, baby," Mama Cheryl mumbled.

Musa could hear the uneasiness in his mama's voice. "Ma, what's wrong? Are you okay?" Musa asked. Silence came over the phone. "Ma," Musa raised his voice.

"A lot is wrong, Musa. I just need you here. Things have started to become messy, Musa."

"Ma, what are you talking about? You have to be more direct, Ma. Please, my phone time is limited," Musa pleaded.

Mama Cheryl let out a deep breath. "It's Ace."

"What about Ace?" Musa asked with concern laced in his voice. "What happened in court today, Ma?"

"They, they requesting the, the death penalty. They trying to kill that girl." Mama Cheryl broke down in tears.

The words "death penalty" hit Musa's chest hard. At that very moment, he wanted to lash out at someone. His protectiveness for Ace kicked in, but the realization that he couldn't protect Ace from her situation hurt him more than receiving the news that the State of Maryland was trying to execute Ace. Musa took in a deep breath and exhaled heavily.

"What the lawyer talking about, Ma?" Musa asked.

Mama Cheryl wiped tears from her eyes and snot from her running nose. "The lawyer said it's still early in the case and the government still could come back and remove the death penalty off the table. But right now, the courts will appoint Ace another attorney, which specializes in death penalty cases. The lawyer would assist Ms. Stoner in defending Ace."

"Naw, fuck that, Ma. We not trusting no fucking lawyer that the government throw our way. Get with Ms. Stoner. Have her the best lawyer out there. I don't give a fuck if the lawyer has to fly in from outta state. We have the money to do it."

"Okay, I will call the lawyer soon as I'm off the phone with you," Mama Cheryl replied. "There is something else I need to tell you, Musa. I'm only telling you because I'm scared, Musa."

Once again, Musa could hear the apprehensiveness in his mother's voice.

"Ma, I'ma need you to tell me what's up. I'ma need to get off this phone soon," Musa stated. He needed some time to think.

"He been coming past my apartment. He's been past here three times, and all three times, I acted like I wasn't home. But all of a sudden, you go to prison, Ace tells me not to trust Brim, and now he's at my door," Mama yammered.

Mama Cheryl was talking so fast. But when his Mama mentioned Brim's name, he put it all together, and now he was a different kind of mad. Musa wanted to kill something, and he preferred that it was Brim.

"Mama, listen to me. I want you to hire a packing company to come in and pack up your whole apartment. Put everything in storage. Then I want you to go get the Porsche Taycan out of storage, take a couple of hundred thousand, and hit the road. Go see your sister in ATL, spend some time with them. You and her both fly out to Cali and visit your best friend. And from there, I want you to buy a flight anywhere in the world and go enjoy yourself."

"No, I can't leave in a time like this."

"Ma, please, just listen to me. Get the lawyer for Ace, pack up, and hit the road. I will be home in three months. I love you," Musa said, hanging up the phone, with his thoughts heavy, and without telling his mom that Ace was his sister.

Jibril Williams

Chapter 6

"Mafia Magic, Mafia Magic! All day, every day," a young kid announced on the block, alerting the fiends that the trap was open and ready for business. It was like the fiends were in every crack and crevice of the block because, in a matter of minutes, the block was crowded with dope fiends that were craving that early morning high.

You could always tell the shooters from the sniffers. Those who chose to inject their veins with the poison always looked bad, with beat up hands and legs swollen, with abscesses from misfiring the dope in their veins. Their clothes were dirty, and shoes were busted. But those who chose to intake the drug through their noses were a little more decent in their appearance.

Bagz took inventory of this from behind the wheel of his 2021 black on black 1500 Dodge Ram. Hell-Cat sat in the passenger seat with a Draco on his lap. His eyes stayed roaming the block. Over the short few months, they both had been blessed in the game. A potent product had been dropped off in their laps. Shoota had given them some heroin that sat blaze to the west side of Baltimore. Niggas throughout the city of Charm had been fucking with them on the dope. But Bagz and Hell-Cat were feeding them niggas with a long handle spoon. They had a system. They would only sell to those who were outside of West Baltimore no less than three ounces. Outside of that, you had to cop the Mafia in wholesale and resell it.

Niggas were mad, but what the fuck could they do? Bagz and Hell-Cat controlled the drugs, so they had the power. The only problem Bagz and Hell-Cat had was they hadn't seen Shoota in months. Shoota hit them off with a package to sell for him. He disappeared when the package got low. Some Mexican chick contacted them on Shoota's behalf to set up a meeting. When they got to the meeting place, the Mexican chick showed up with the product, collected Shoota's money, and kept it moving, leaving them a number to contact for more product.

Bagz and Hell-Cat were seeing some major money now. They were running the traps like they were 7-11 convenience stores. They were open 24-7. The only time they closed was when the jump-outs or the Narcotics Task Force was rolling heavy through the blocks.

Bagz and Hell-Cat weren't slow to the game. They had spent many times on the sidelines, watching other mutha-fuckas getting money and watching others build small empires, just to have them fall in six months. They were taking precaution on every corner. The trap houses were equipped with radio scanners, so they could always hear what Twelve was doing, plotting, and planning. Four lookouts were posted on each corner. Six shooters stayed on the block at all times, protecting the works and the product.

"What we getting into after we finish making our rounds?" Hell-Cat asked, as he turned the Meek Mill track down on the truck's radio.

"Shid, fool, you tell me?" Bagz stated, slightly distracted.

He sat up in the truck's driver seat, when he saw the three heavy duty GMC Denali trucks bend the corner. He tapped Hell-Cat's leg, alerting him.

"Fools," he yelled out.

The whole block started to scatter like roaches. The look-out was screaming, "Twelve!"

The shooter fell back into the trenches. Hell-Cat's phone rang. It was the shooter on the roof.

-"Yeah?" Hell-Cat said when he answered.

"Twelve creeping, you good down there, or you want us to air their asses out so you and Bagz can hit it on them?" The shooter asked, a little too excitedly.

"Hold fast, let's see what they do," Bagz said, speaking for Hell-Cat.

Bagz's phone vibrated, and he answered. "Who this?"

A raspy voice came through the phone. "Shoota. Where you at? I'm on the block."

"That's you in the black truck coming through like you the Feds?" Bagz asked.

"Where you at?" Shoota replied, without answering Bagz's question.

"Me and Hell-Cat sitting in the Ram 1500."

The phone was disconnected and the GMC's pulled up next to the truck.

"Tell them niggas to fall back on the roof," Bagz ordered when he stepped out of the Ram. He saw Shoota getting out of the middle GMC truck, dressed in wheat-colored Timbs, black Louie jeans, and a wheat-color shirt that was covered by a bullet-proof vest. The Double M chain around his neck was flashy.

"Wassup, Shoota? Man, where the fuck you been?" Bagz asked as he embraced Shoota in a hug. "Damn, you popping up on a nigga, dressed like 50 Cent, bullet-proof vest and shit. Nigga, what's good."

"Man, so much shit happened. But listen, I need to holla at you and Hell-Cat," Shoota said.

"Yeah, we can get in the truck, or we can go somewhere and holla," Bagz informed.

"The truck is good-"

"Papi, I see that you forgot about me already," a pouty Emma said from the back of the Denali, which Shoota had just exited. She held the door open, sitting in the backseat, looking like one of them sexy news reporters that you see often.

"Never would I forget about you. But I need you to sit tight for me, while I holla at the good men."

Emma gave him a look of disappointment. And he hated how that look made him feel. It was Emma that held him after being pulled from his car, when he crashed after Papaya sent a shooter to end his life. Without Emma, he probably wouldn't be standing where he was today. He beckoned her with his head, telling her to come on. She happily exited the GMC, wearing a white pair of Chanel jeans, and the fire engine red stilettos wrapped perfectly around her pretty toes. The heels allowed her toes to be seen. Toenails painted in red matched her red Chanel belt and lipstick. She straightened out her white Chanel button-up shirt.

Shoota held the Ram's cab door open for Emma. One of the GMC's pulled off and parked at the end of the block. And the GMC that was tailing the caravan backed the truck up and posted up at the other end of the street.

Bagz checked Emma. This woman was so exotic. He wondered if she was the plug, or just a bitch Shoota had moving work for him. As soon as all parties were safely in the truck, you could hear the magic chant. *Mafia Magic, Mafia Magic, all day every day.* And just that quickly, the block came back to life.

Shoota, Emma, Hell-Cat, and Bagz watched the traffic flow. The sight was intriguing to Emma. She'd never seen her product move on this lower level before. She was so used to seeing the work move on a larger scale. In her mind, to get out and go hand to hand on a street corner, on a poverty-stricken block, really was beneath he. But it made her respect them more because it took a special type of person to overcome the hardship and rise to power. That was another reason why she stuck with Shoota, he was a lion in a jungle. He outshined all the others.

"So, you gonna tell me where you been, fam?" Bagz asked, for a second time.

Shoota made eye contact with Bagz in the rearview mirror. Anger flashed in Shoota's eyes. "A weak muthafucka tried to take me out. I got hit two times in the neck and shoulder."

Hearing that news made Bagz and Hell-Cat turn around in their seats and face Shoota. Both of them held concern in their eyes. And there was no doubt, if Shoota needed them to ride for him, they would.

"That's not why I'm here. I'm here because I want to take Money Mafia to another level. I want to plug the whole east coast. I want the whole east coast to be pushing Sinaloa Cartel product. We expanding Money Mafia through the city of B-More. I want us on every block on the East Baltimore streets. Then, from there, we pushing farther into Maryland."

Bagz and Hell-Cat were feeling the movement Shoota was preaching. They both were inching to get started.

"I don't want you out here in these streets going to war with these niggas. If a muthafucka not trying to get down with Money Mafia, don't trip, we send in professional hittas from Mexico. We only focusing on growing the profit and expanding the family. From now on, hit me from this phone." Shoota handed Bagz a burner phone.

Emma's panties moisten over, listening to Shoota command his foot soldiers. She liked when men took charge that would only lead to her making more money. Emma had been wrestling with the idea of sleeping with Shoota. She hadn't made up her mind as of now, but she was close to making her decision.

"I got some other business to attend to, but I will be back through soon, so we could hit a club up, or something. But in the meantime, keep pushing the product and the Mafia," Shoota said, opening the door of the truck. He got out and extended his hand to Emma to help her out of the truck.

She nodded her head to Hell-Cat and Bagz, before getting in the waiting GMC. Shoota tapped the Double M chain around his neck and mouthed Money Mafia at his two loyal men, before getting in the truck behind Emma. And just like that, Shoota was gone.

Chapter 7

Jus-Blaze sat on the patio of his three-bedroom home, while he nursed a glass of Hennessy in his hand and puffed on a blunt. He was weighing the pros and cons of his situation. Brim didn't give a fuck about the Mafia the way Musa did. He understood every leadership would be different, but loyalty should always be the foundation of every street organization.

Brim wasn't demonstrating loyalty towards Musa, nor the Money Mafia family itself, by merging the families together. Musa would definitely be opposed to the merge. Jus-Blaze knew Musa never liked Pop-Roc, nor the caliber of niggas that associated with him. Jus-Blaze blew smoke in the air as the fall breeze took the smoke away.

Jus-Blaze's thoughts turned to Sharkhead and Stink, and he became angry. All they were concerned about was money. If a man placed money over loyalty, then they were not worth protecting their honor. Jus-Blaze sipped from the glass of Henny, before plucking ashes from his blunt on the patio and making his way inside his home. He had some planning to do.

***

"Ooooh! Pop-Roc, Shiiiiiit!" A project thick chick by the name of Cash App moaned and bucked back on Pop-Roc's wood, which he was feeding her doggy style.

Pop-Roc stood behind Cash App with her cheek spread wide open for the camera's view. He was giving Cash App his best shots. Even though she was moaning and screaming like Pop-Roc had the biggest dick in the world, she was taking the wood like a champ.

Pop-Roc had found Cash App on BackPage. He hit her up and she fell through to make her first appearance on

ButtBusters. Pop-Roc slowed his strokes down and let a glob of spit spill from his mouth onto Cash App's asshole. He pushed his thumb in her butt, using his saliva as lubricant.

"Ooooh, put another finger in it. I need two fingers in my booty," Cash App announced, as her ass splashed even wetter.

Her request was met by Pop-Roc by removing his thumb and replacing it with his middle and pointer finger.

"Ooooh, shiiit, yes!" Cash App cried out and started pushing back hard on Pop-Roc's wood and fingers.

Pop-Roc looked in the camera and screamed out. "Shit!" Pop-Roc moaned loudly.

The camera crew started laughing because the young freak was too much for Pop-Roc. He came out her pussy and jumped dead in Cash App's ass with one swift motion. Pop-Roc was in her bowels, but it felt like a whole new pussy. To Cash App, it was the same dick because she bounced back on Pop-Roc's pipe, like it was nothing. She tightened her sphincter. Pop-Roc gritted his teeth. Cash App's ass was on point like a muthafucka. He dug his fingers into the thickness of her ass cheeks and pounded away.

Cash App was loving every thrust Pop-Roc was giving her. Pop-Roc always heard that a woman could cum from being fucked in the ass. He always thought that was a myth, but once he had seen Cash App cream up around his pipe, he knew the myth was nothing but the truth. The visual made his penis erupt. He pulled out of Cash App's asshole and splashed his load all in the crack of her ass. His nut came out thick and white. Cash App reached between her legs, inserted two fingers into her wet pussy, and her body shook violently.

The ButtBusters camera crew caught all the action, and then cut the cameras.

Brim walked into the hotel room, catching the last five minutes of the action. Being a porn star wasn't really his thing, but Pop-Roc seemed too deeply into it. When Pop-Roc brought on the idea about the Amateur porn company, Brim was reluctant, but he gave it a shot and dropped some money into the ButtBusters company. To his surprise, he made a hell of a profit.

Pop-Roc got out of the bed and went to the bathroom. The next group of up and coming porn stars took their places on the bed and started performing oral on each other in the sixty-nine position.

Pop-Roc walked out of the bathroom barefooted and shirt-less, with a pair of black Versace jeans on and a burning Back-wood hanging from his lips.

"Wassup, Slim," Pop-Roc said in a whisper, as he dapped Brim up. He wanted to keep his voice low so the sound mic wouldn't pick his voice up and interrupt the foreplay that was taking place in front of the cameras.

"Just breezing through," Brim replied.

Pop-Roc motioned for Brim to follow him. He led Brim to the adjoined room, where there was extra equipment stored along with bottles of D'Usse and a pile of weed on the table. Pop-Roc grabbed a bottle of D'Usse and drank straight from the bottle.

"We need to meet tomorrow. The shipment is coming in. We need to be prompt and ready to go. I don't trust these Mexicans. I still don't know if Musa figured shit out yet, but we need to be on our P's and Q's when we meet to get the work," Brim said, picking a bud out of the pile of weed and busting it down to prepare it to be rolled in the Backwood.

"I'm gonna be ready, Brim. But I don't think Musa has a clue to the double cross that was put down on him. If he did, he wouldn't be co-signing with the plug to deliver the shipment," Pop-Roc stated.

Since Brim had taken control of Money Mafia and joined forces with Pop-Roc, the two had a sit-down, and Brim revealed his past and situation with Musa to Pop-Roc.

"After we secure the work, we will plan how and when we gonna merge the families. We need to make sure that we're united under the same umbrella," Brim said, putting some heat to the neatly rolled Backwood.

"Speaking of that, playboy, my people are not opposing a united front, but I want to confirm, or should I say, get a clear understanding with you. I'm requesting, after the merge, that we go fifty-fifty down the middle." Before Brim could interject, Pop-Roc held up a hand, stopping him. "I understand that the plug is yours. So, after we complete the shipment we are about to receive, I would only start looking for the split on the next load. And on that load, I will put up half for the shipment."

Brim sat on the sofa and stared at the Backwood that burned slowly in his hand. Hearing Pop-Roc wanted a fifty-fifty split had him feeling a certain way. He felt that Pop-Roc should have accepted the sixty-forty split. A nigga ain't even in the door yet, and he already want to up the size of the pie. A perpetual greedy nigga. But Brim had a plan.

"I'm good with the 50/50 split, but you also have the responsibility to pay half on Musa's cut. This is only until we can find a plug for ourselves," Brim said, looking at Pop-Roc.

Now it was time for Pop-Roc to feel a certain way because he didn't factor in Musa's cut. But he couldn't back out now because he had his own plans. Pop-Roc reached over and dapped Brim up, securing the agreement.

Brim stood to his feet. "I got to go holla at some people. So, I'm gonna holla later."

"Come on, Slim, don't bounce yet. I got some twins coming through for a few sex scenes. Let's bust down these bitches," Pop-Roc stated excitedly.

"Naw, Slim, I'm a drug dealer, not a porn star," Brim replied.

"Brim, we have a porn company. You have to experience the fruits from it," Pop-Roc said.

"Not my M.O., but I do need you to get on something. I need you to have someone to scope out an address for me," Brim spoke seriously.

"Okay, give me the run down," Pop-Roc replied.

"It's Musa's mom. I think she knows I put shit in the game on Musa. She has been avoiding me. So, I need someone to watch her place for a few days. And if they see her, give me a call. I just need to know if she up to something."

"Alright, got it. Just text me the address and I will put someone on it," Pop-Roc said with his mental wheels turning.

"Okay, I will. Be safe, Slim," Brim said, dapping Pop-Roc up and making his exit.

Pop-Roc sat down on the sofa, thinking this was the break he really needed.

Chapter 8

Ace's hands trembled as she dialed Musa's number. She was praying that he had his phone and he could talk. It had been three days since she made her court appearance and found out that the State of Maryland was seeking the death penalty. She knew that Musa was aware of her situation because she had talked to Mama Cheryl and she'd told her she conveyed the bad news to Musa.

The phone rang three times before Musa answered. Ace's heart was beating fast. The jail pre-recording kicked in, reciting that the person was calling from jail and the call was subject to be monitored. The recording also explained that, in order to talk to the inmate, the recipient must press 1. Musa pressed 1 without hesitation.

"My number one," Musa said into the phone. And Ace's heart melted, like a block of ice sitting on top of a warm stove.

"Hi, baby," Ace whispered. Water came to her eyes.

"How you holding up in there?" Musa asked. He already knew Ace's state.

"They trying to kill a real one, Mo. They trying to X your number one out the game."

"Don't even start thinking that it's gonna be an easy task for them to do. I don't give a fuck if I got to pour all of Double M's resources into getting you free, that's what I'm gonna do. So, know that it's Money Mafia, all day every day."

"I know, but I'm scared, Musa. I don't want to die in prison, baby."

"And you not gonna die in prison," Musa said. He kind of regretted the words he'd just spoken out of his mouth, because he wasn't sure how Ace's situation would turn out. All he knew was that he was going to do his best to get her free.

"Now, have you been eating?" Musa asked, changing the subject.

"Much as I can. The food from the Mess Hall is pure garbage. So, my meals consist of commissary food. I mostly eat tuna, Ramen noodles, and Ritz crackers."

"The tuna is high in protein and the noodles and crackers will put weight on you, so that's good. How are your wounds healing?" Musa asked.

"They are good. They are healing. I'm still experiencing some pain, but my strength is growing." Ace sniffled.

Musa knew that he didn't have long on the phone with Ace. There was only fifteen minutes per call.

"Ace, I have a few things to tell you, before the phone disconnects us. I got a letter from the Parole Commissioner. They are reinstating my parole. Not to go into too much detail, they stated something about Mr. Braxton being corrupt. So, they are letting me go in about ninety days."

Excitement shot through Ace. She was happy that Musa was going to get out soon. But quickly, a cloud of sadness came over her. Ace realized she wouldn't be home to be with Musa.

"Wow, Musa, that's what's up, baby," Ace stated.

Musa could hear the sadness in Ace's tone. "Ace, nothing is gonna change with us. Ace-"

"But I'm going to prison, Musa, and I don't want you waiting on me. Find someone that's going to make you happy."

"Ace, you talking crazy as fuck, baby. It's you that I want, and it's you that I'm gonna be with. Once I'm out, I'll be able to help you get out. Get your heart and mind off the negative bullshit and focus on the fight we have in front of you." Musa started getting a little frustrated with Ace's mindset.

Before Ace could respond, Musa moved on to his next topic. He didn't want to mention the situation about him being her brother and them sharing the same father, but he knew he had to. "There's something I need to tell you."

Now it was Ace's turn to hear Musa's voice change. Ace could tell it was bad, so she mentally braced herself. "What's going on, Musa?" Ace asked.

Musa sighed before he started talking. "I had the opportunity to meet your father."

Creases spread across Ace's forehead, after hearing Musa's statement. "Musa, I don't think that's possible. My father is dead, and has been dead for a very long time."

"Naw, Ace, he's alive. He's dying, but as of right now, he's alive," Musa replied.

"That can't be possible, Musa. My mother told me that my father died. She also told me he didn't want me as his daughter because I was into women. So, why we even talking about this?"

"Ace, the story that your Mom told you about your Dad being dead was a lie. Your father abandoned you because his upbringing frowned upon same-sex relationships."

"Musa, you talking like you know something. What is it you trying to tell me, Musa?"

"I'm trying to tell you that you're my sister. We share the same biological father, Ace," Musa yammered.

A dead silence fell over the phone. The only thing that could be heard was Ace's heavy breathing through the phone.

"Musa, please tell me that you're on some sick bullshit," Ace mumbled.

"I wish I was, Ace, but it's the truth. Our father is here with me. He wants to talk to you, Ace. He wants to rekindle the daughter and father relationship."

"My mother told me he was dead," Ace stated in anger.

"But he's not, Ace. He's here in Wackin Hunt Prison, serving a life sentence. He's dying, Ace. He wants to talk to you and explain his action-"

"Fuck him, Musa. That muthafucka abandoned me and my mom. He wasn't there to protect me from my stepbrother. He wasn't there to make sure my mother died comfortably, when she suffered from cancer. That bitch cut me out his life when my mother told him I was showing interest in girls," Ace screamed through the phone at Musa.

Musa let out a sigh. He just wanted to get Moses on the phone so he would have the task of explaining why he wasn't there for his daughter.

"Ace, I think you should really hear pops out first, before you write the man all the way out of your life."

"Musa, I don't give a fuck what he got to say. I don't care if I had to confess my sins to him before I'm permitted into heaven, I won't say shit to him. And when you talk to him, tell him that I, his only daughter, said fuck him with a great, big, fat dick."

"You have one minute remaining on this call," the jail phone announced, letting Ace know her time with Musa was at an end.

"Ace, please think about it. I know you mad, but-"

"Musa, I already spoke my peace about the situation. I got to go. I love you," Ace replied, cutting Musa off. She didn't want to hear anything that Musa had to say about their father.

Musa sighed. "I love you, too."

Musa hung up the phone with Ace. For some reason, his inner self was advising him that he shouldn't have told Ace that he was her brother, nor the fact that their father was alive. A part of him was feeling like he was causing her more harm than good. He was upset with his father for putting him in this situation. Musa knew how Ace felt about him, and she wasn't in a position to have any of her dreams shattered. He still couldn't believe Ace was his sister.

Musa shook his head from side to side, as he stashed his phone in its hiding spot and laid back on his bunk. His mental was heavy, he needed to think.

Chapter 9

Ace didn't feel better after talking to Musa, like she normally did. She was angry as fuck. She could feel the warmth in her chest from her anger and stress. She navigated through the unit until she found her cell. She was happy to find it empty of Tammy. Her cellmate had become a comfort to her, since she'd been in the county jail. But Ace wasn't ready to repeat the conversation she'd just had with Musa to Tammy.

Ace grabbed her shower gear and headed to the shower. She was hoping that a hot shower would calm the storm that was brewing within her. The news of Musa being her brother was something hard for her to absorb, mentally. Ace wanted to cuss her father out. She wanted to scream at him and tell him all her pains, and make him feel like shit. But she would never give him the satisfaction of hearing her voice, nor hearing the tears in her voice.

Ace got in the shower and hung her shower bag on the hook. The shower bag contained everything a woman in jail needed to shower and groom herself. She stripped down and turned the water on. She stepped under the showerhead and let the warm water splash over her head and cascade down her body.

Ace didn't feel anything for her father's situation. She didn't care that he was in prison for life. She didn't care that he was dying. Ace felt he was getting everything he deserved. Ace didn't give a fuck that her deadbeat dad was dying. She saw the situation through a different set of lenses. It was her dad's fault that she should love Musa as a brother, but would only view Musa as a lover. Even after finding out Musa was her brother, her feelings for him hadn't changed. She was still craving for his touches and kisses. Ace felt like her father had taken that away.

Ace could not forget the last time she had seen her father. She closed her eyes and the memories came flooding back, like an ocean wave rolls in on a beach.

***

Ace was sitting on the sofa, watching reruns of The Walking Dead. Her mom was in the kitchen preparing dinner, chicken, red beans, and rice. She and her mom had just had a long discussion about the phone call her mom had gotten earlier from her school's principal. Her principal called her mother and informed her that Ace had gotten caught kissing another little girl that attended her school. Ace got suspended from school for three days.

Ace's mom didn't do what other moms would have done. Instead of her mother going off on her and belittling her, her mother had a sit-down with her and explained to her that she understood what Ace was feeling and going through. Her mom explained to her that she once had interests in women, when she was growing up. Her mother told her she would love her and support her, but she couldn't support her displaying her interest of girls in school. And Ace understood clearly that she couldn't ever do what she did at school again. Ace was feeling good about the conversation she'd had with her mother.

A knock came to the door, drawing Ace's attention from The Walking Dead.

"Ace, baby, get the door," her mother yelled from the kitchen, the aroma of her cooking smelling like a feast.

"Who is it?" Ace asked through the door.

"Your daddy, baby girl," Moses's voice came through the door.

Ace's heart came to life. She was a daddy's girl. Her dad didn't come around much, but when he did, he showed her mad love, treated her like a princess. And Ace loved every moment of it.

"Dad," Ace screamed, unlocking the door and swinging it open.

Standing on the other side was her dad, Moses, looking tall and strong, wearing a bright smile. Ace jumped into her father's arms, and she wrapped her skinny legs around his waist. Ace's dad hugged her with a hug of love and warmth. He held her there and absorbed his daughter. Moses's cologne was inhaled by Ace's little nose. She loved how good her dad smelled.

"Ace, who's at the door?" Ace's mom stopped in mid-sentence. Her eyes were trained on Moses and Ace. She hadn't seen Moses in six months.

Moses put Ace down and spoke to his daughter's mother. "Hello!"

"And hello to you. We weren't expecting you," Ace's mom said. She was displeased with how Moses came in and out of her daughter's life as he pleased. She gave Moses the evil eye.

"You're never expecting me, but I'm here, so now what?" Moses said with a slight smile on his face.

He and the woman standing in front of him never had the best relationship. She wanted to turn Moses into a husband, but Moses was nothing but an Outlaw. Moses stayed on the move, as if the law was in hot pursuit of him. The only thing that kept him coming around was Ace.

"Can I see you in the kitchen for a minute?" Pam said.

"Baby girl, I will be right back. Let me talk to your mama real quick. And when I come back, I want you to meet somebody," Moses said tenderly to, Ace as he walked behind Pam into the small kitchen.

"What is it, Pam?" Moses said, getting to the point. He dug in his pocket and pulled out a stack of bills.

She was reluctant to accept the money he was handing to her. But she did, and pushed the stack into her back pocket.

"Listen, you need to spend more time with Ace. Popping up every few months, baring gifts and money doesn't make up for your absence. You missed that girl's birthday two months ago!"

"What the fuck you want me to do, Pam? You know what type of man I am. You knew from the jump the lifestyle I was living when you met me."

"And that same lifestyle has been producing the same results, an absent father, out of your daughter's life. Moses, if you are not rich by now from fucking around in them streets, then it's time for you to come on in off them streets," Pam said, snaking her neck with her hands on her hips.

Moses was offended by the fact that just rolled off of Pam's tongue. "Bitch, watch your mouth," Moses warned.

"If you spend some time with that girl, maybe she wouldn't be interested in girls." Pam didn't take heed to Moses's warning.

Moses balled up his face up in a mask of ugliness. "Fuck you talking about? My daughter ain't no fucking coochie licker."

Moses grabbed Pam by the neck. She clawed at his hand to release her. Tears flooded her eyes.

"The school called me and told me Ace was caught kissing another girl today," Pam said, fighting to breathe.

Moses let Pam go. He was mentally fucked up about the news of his daughter kissing another girl. In the islands of Jamaica, these types of actions were frowned upon.

"I know you beat her fucking ass," Moses suggested.

"What a beating going to do? It's not my job to beat her for being attracted to who she's attracted to. It's my job to guide her and love her, no matter who she loves or is attracted to." Pam stated firmly.

Moses searched her eyes for sarcasm. And when he found none, he back handed her. Slap! Pam fell to the floor.

"Bitch, you got my daughter lickin' pussy. She didn't pick that shit up outta nowhere," Moses yelled, kicking Pam in the thigh.

"Arrggh," she yelled.

Moses grabbed her by the hair and slapped her face for the second time. Ace heard the commotion and ran into the kitchen, catching her daddy bringing his big hand across her mother's face.

"Stop, daddy, stop," Ace yelled, running and grabbing her father's extended arm, stopping him from hitting her mother.

"Get the fuck off me!" Moses spoke with venom in his voice, scaring Ace half to death.

"Ace, get outta here, baby. Go outside, baby, go," Pam yelled.

Ace didn't want to leave her mother, but she was so afraid. She ran out the apartment and took a seat on the front porch of her building. Tears rolled down her eyes. She had never seen her dad hit her mom before, and the sight placed her in panic mode.

Ace looked up and saw a boy sitting in a truck, staring at her. Even though she was sad, something in her compelled her to wave at him, and he waved back. Ace heard the building door open, and her father stepped out, staring at her with hateful eyes and mumbling.

The words, "Hoe, just like your mama," came out his mouth.

Ace watched her father get into the truck and pull away from her building. Ace sat there with a crushed spirit.

***

Ace's mind came back from memory lane. The water from the shower hid her tears. Reliving that experience made her hate her father even more. She made up her mind. She would never talk to him again. Ace grabbed her Dove bar and washed her body.

Chapter 10

It had been days since Musa had heard from Ace, and he would admit, he was sick over it. He felt like shit, for sure, and borderline ill was what he indeed was feeling.

"My sister," he mumbled to himself for like the umpteenth time since he learned that that his queen, the woman he has fallen in love with, was in fact his sibling. He was still processing the reality of such info.

"My fucking sister," he mumbled again, that time with much more intensity.

His anger was surfacing, as he thought of the feelings he truly felt for Ace, and the fact that such feelings were not morally allowed to exist for one that shares the same bloodline as you. No, there was just no way the woman he could not stop dreaming and fantasizing about, shit, the woman he could picture sexing, fucking, to keep it all the way real, was in fact his sibling, his sister.

"My fucking sister," he said to himself, once again, in a muffled tone. He leaned back against the brick wall, as he laid on his cell bunk. He closed his eyes, as thoughts of not only Ace, consumed his mental, but his father as well.

Although, Ace was angry at their father for withholding such a crucial truth, he, however, felt differently. He loved his father, and yes, he felt some type of way at first, but he no longer held a grudge for keeping the truth from him.

Speaking of his father, he decided to give him a call in that moment. Perhaps a talk with him would take his mind off of Ace. Since their last conversation, he had not reached out to him.

He knew Ace was upset at learning the truth, but not making contact was not what either needed in the present moment. They needed each other. At least he needed her, and most of all, he needed to figure out a plan to get her out of the current situation she was in. Despite learning the truth, she was still his queen, his heart, and there was no way he would allow her to undergo the death penalty. No fucking way. Not while he was breathing.

Shaking his head at the current dilemma, he reached into his private stash spot and retrieved his cell phone. He wasted no time dialing his father's cell number, only to receive no answer. Seconds later, he redialed the number, and once more, no answer.

Figuring his father was occupied, he made a mental note to try calling again in an hour or so.

As the time passed, his father's words echoed in his mental.

"Musa, if you can't turn that shit off like a light switch, then you need to knock the light bulb out that bitch, because no son of mine is fucking with his sister."

"Damn," he mumbled, once more, at the brief memory. He then shook his head again.

"Easier said than fucking done."

"Knocking the light bulb out that bitch," as his father put it, was easier said than done. Learning that Ace was, in fact, his sister, did not change or suppress his feelings for her. He wanted her, just the same. His love for her existed, just the same.

I need to get my queen out, and that is on everything I love.

While counting the minutes before he called his father again, thoughts of Ace flooded his mental, while a plan to make her dilemma disappear formed, almost like a dramatic slide show.

His determination surfaced, just then. His queen was coming home by any means necessary.

Chapter 11

"You need to let your son know that you are not doing too well."

Silence filled the space between them before he looked up. His eyes met the prison's nurse. The look of concern was noticeable in her eyes. He wanted to appreciate her act of kindness, but at the present moment, he was surely in his feelings.

"He knows already," Moses replied to the woman's suggestion.

"You know what I mean. You need to let him know that your cancer has reached its last stage and that you don't have much time. Avoiding him is not going to make things better."

More silence filled the space in between them, before the nurse spoke again.

"Do you hear me?"

"Yeah, I hear you."

"Good. You're clear to go back to your cell. I'll call in for transport."

Letting out a sigh, Moses watched as the nurse left the small room located in the nurse's office. He closed his eyes as he leaned his head against the brick wall. He was seated in a small chair, the same one he had been resting in for the last three hours. After feeling terribly fatigued, he was brought in to the nurse to receive medical attention. He rested for about an hour on a similar version of a bunk, before retiring to the small chair, where he was currently seated.

He sighed, once again, as he gathered his thoughts. The nurse's words echoed in his head, as his thoughts switched to his son. He did need to alert Musa of his current condition, but more thoughts crossed his mind suddenly.

"Ace," he mumbled to himself, as he reopened his eyes.

He raised his head and stared straight ahead at nothing in particular. Just the thought of his only daughter at odds with him caused an unsettling feeling he could not shake. And in that moment, he decided that, before he left this earth, he would not only get right with her, but he would make sure she was straight, by any means.

"I have to get her the fuck out of there," he mumbled, just as two officers entered the room. Moses' time arrived to return to his cell, and he looked forward to it. The first task on his agenda was to call Musa, since he was sure he was worried by then.

Plus, a plan had to be set in motion, and he needed his son to execute it, like never before.

***

After returning to his cell, Moses headed straight to his stash spot and retrieved his cell phone. Securing his surroundings, he dialed Musa's number. The phone rang a total of three times, before Musa's voice was heard.

Musa's instant questions caused a sigh to escape Moses' lips. He rubbed his temple before he finally spoke.

"Listen, I have some shit up with me that I need to put you on game. But first shit first, we need to get Ace the fuck out of there, and we need to get that shit done ASAP."

Chapter 12

"I can't believe I got this whole apartment packed up and ready to be placed in storage in three days," Mama Cheryl thought to herself as she made her last rounds through her apartment to make sure that she wasn't leaving anything behind. She had hired a moving company to help her pack her belongings and take them to storage. The moving crew had just taken the last box to the truck.

There was nothing left in her bedroom but some hangers in the closet. Mama Cheryl made her way to the bathroom and it was empty. She flushed the toilet for good measure. Her last stop was the kitchen. The cabinets under and over the top of the sink were empty. She remembered she was supposed to call Musa to let him know she was leaving the apartment and heading to the storage. From there, she would be hitting the highway, going straight to Atlanta to visit her sister, Patty. It had been a long time since she had spent some time with her sister, and it was way overdue for them to rekindle their bond.

Mama Cheryl called Musa's phone, but it went straight to voicemail, indicating that he had his phone powered off. She sent him a quiet text, letting him know she was leaving the apartment. She hated the fact that Brim was snooping around her apartment. She was never a fan of how Musa was living. She knew the life that he lived could always bring trouble to her doorstep. This was one of the reasons his father, Moses, stayed in the wind. He claimed that he didn't want to bring any trouble to Musa and her. Although Mama Cheryl knew there was more to it, she accepted it.

Musa was her only child, and she was going to stand by him, no matter what came her way. So, if Musa wanted her to pack up and move, she would, without complaint. Many times, Musa stood by her. He never stopped loving her, when she was an addict. He never complained about the harsh living conditions and lack of food and clothes because she spent money on drugs to get high. Mama Cheryl loved her only child. She would even kill for him, if she had to.

Mama Cheryl opened the fridge. It was empty, except for a stick of butter and a box of baking soda. She sat the phone on top of the fridge, removed the items, and kicked the fridge door closed with her foot.

"Ms. Cheryl, the truck is all packed up," the moving guy, whose name was Charles, stated.

Mama Cheryl jumped. "Man, you scared the hell out of me."

"I'm so sorry, ma'am!" Charles sincerely apologized.

"That's okay, young man. I'm ready," Mama stated, following Charles out of the apartment, locking the door behind her.

Mama Cheryl walked to Musa's Porsche. She knew the car was too fast for her liking, but when she pulled up on her sister Patty, she wanted to make a statement, as if she had her shit all the way together. She got into the Porsche and led the way to the storage unit.

**

Pepper sat restlessly behind the wheel of his GMC. He couldn't believe that Pop-Roc had him stalking this old ass broad. He wondered what the play was. Pop-Roc always had angles he was playing. He picked the phone up and dialed Pop-Roc's number.

"What you got?" Roc asked, answering the phone on the second ring. Pepper could hear moaning, like someone was having sex, in the background. Pepper knew Pop-Roc was at one of the Butt Buster sets, making porn. He wanted to attend one bad. But Pop-Roc always denied him access.

"Man, this broad is moving. She packing her shit and moving. She got a whole fucking moving company."

"Fuck, okay, stay with that bitch. Find out where she going." Pop-Roc had no intentions on calling Brim. The way Pop-Roc figured, if Musa didn't trust anybody, he trusted his mama. He knew Musa was worth a few million. If Musa was locked up, then his mother had access to that money.

"All right, got you, big homie."

"Pepper, don't fuck this up. This your chance to move up. If you get a chance, snatch the bitch and bring her to me."

"Say less, Pop-Roc. I'm on it," Pepper said, canceling the call and jumping behind the moving company truck.

***

"Thank you all so much," Mama Cheryl said, handing Charles an envelope with his fee in it. Then she handed him, and his two crew members, a crispy one hundred dollar bill a piece. She knew the tip was big, but she was for supporting black business. They each thanked her, and got into their truck and left. Mama Cheryl got into the Porsche and started looking for her phone. She wanted to try Musa again.

"Where the hell is my phone?" She asked herself. Then she remembered she sat it on the fridge at the apartment. She was mad that she had to drive all the way back to the apartment. That was a twenty-five-minute drive. She wanted to get on the road before the rush hour traffic. But, oh well, she was driving a Porsche. So, in her mind, it wasn't going to be that bad.

Mama Cheryl made the drive in 18 minutes flat. She jumped out of the Porsche with that "I have to pee" dance. She grabbed her pocketbook and threw it over her shoulder and ran into the kitchen. She snatched the phone off the fridge and ran into the bathroom.

Pepper pulled his truck up, just in time to see Mama Cheryl grab her pocketbook out of her car and run back into the apartment. This was his chance to snatch her. He hopped out of his truck and speed-walked into the apartment building. He reached Mama Cheryl's door. It was sitting ajar. He pushed the door open to find an empty living room. He went in and closed the door behind him.

Pepper removed the gun that was on his hip. He was thinking that grabbing the old lady with the phat ass was going to be the easiest thing he had done for Pop-Roc. He peeped in the kitchen and no Mama Cheryl. Then he noticed he could hear water running, and that could only leave one place for Mama Cheryl to be, the bathroom. He made his way towards the sound of running water. He entered the hallway, there was a bedroom on the left, and at the end of the hall, there was a bathroom. The door was closed, but you could hear the water running.

Pepper made his move. He quickly walked down the hall with his gun in his hand. He was hoping he would catch the old broad with her pants down, sitting on the toilet. When his hand touched the doorknob, the hair on his neck stood straight up. He felt the cold steel touch the base of his cranium.

"If you breathe too hard, young man, I'll blow the contents of your brain all over that door in front of you. Now slowly drop your gun on the floor."

Immediately a lump formed in Pepper's throat and his mouth became as dry as sandpaper. He followed Mama Cheryl's orders.

Mama Cheryl used her foot to move Pepper's gun behind them. "I wasn't going to hurt you," Pepper said.

"Shut the fuck up! You muthafuckas always talking about you not going to hurt someone when they got the up's on you. Now open the bathroom door."

When Pepper turned the knob and pushed the door open, the sink faucet was running full blast. He then knew Mama Cheryl tricked him.

"Take off your shoes, get in the tub, and put your hands behind your back," Mama Cheryl ordered.

Pepper was reluctant, but he complied with Cheryl's orders. Cheryl immediately worked Pepper's shoestrings out of his black Air Max's. She kept a careful eye on Pepper and her 30 near her.

"This shit ain't that serious," Pepper spoke from the tub.

Mama Cheryl ignored him. She quickly tied Pepper's hands behind his back with one shoestring, then quickly did the same with his ankles. She stood to her feet and pulled the hammer back on her gun.

"Who sent you?" Mama Cheryl asked. She was breathing hard. Her hand shook violently. Pepper could see the gun shaking in her hand. He was afraid the gun was going to go off at any second. No matter how much he loved Oxon Hill Mafia Boyz. Pop-Roc wasn't worth dying for.

"Pop-Roc sent me," Pepper yammered out.

"Who's this Pop-Roc? Why Pop-Roc send you to kill me. Stop lying, Brim sent your ass," Mama Cheryl screamed, placing her finger on the trigger.

"No-no-no. Pop-Roc and Brim are together. All I know is Pop-Roc wanted me to watch you. But then today he told me to grab you and bring you to him."

Now things started to make sense. Brim had been coming around out of the blue. Now this bastard was at her door, trying to bring her harm. Mama Cheryl looked down at the young man that was in her tub. The young man reminded her of Musa when he was his age. But Musa wasn't dumb enough to follow a person in a big ass GMC truck.

"How old are you?" Mama Cheryl asked.

The question struck Pepper as odd. But he answered. "I'm 19," Pepper replied.

Cheryl closed her eyes and shook her head. She uncocked her gun. She knew the young man was a baby, trapped in a man's world.

"Listen, baby, on any other day like today, you would have been dead. But today, God touched my heart. What's your name, baby?"

When Pepper heard the statement that God touched her heart. He knew he was going to live. "They call me Pepper."

"Okay, I will let my son know that. But I'm not sure if God is going to touch his heart about you trying to hurt his mama. So, I advise you, when you get loose, to run," Mama Cheryl said, walking out of the bathroom.

She left the apartment door open to make it easy for someone to find Pepper. When she got into the Porsche, she checked her hair in the mirror, pushed a pair of Chanel shades onto her face, and put her apartment complex in her rearview.

Chapter 13

"When we going to sit down for a game of chess? It's only a meeting of the minds over a battlefield," Papaya stated humbly, as he and Musa walked the track of the yard.

"Or just murder among friends," Musa retorted. The statement caused Papaya's feet to grow heavy and stop. He searched Musa's face for troubled water. But he saw none. So, he pushed forward.

"That's such a wicked statement, Musa. What brings such words?" Papaya inquired.

A smile fell on Musa's face. "Papaya, you take all joking and non-joking statements too seriously."

"There's always some truth in a joke," Papaya refuted.

"The life that we live has desensitized you, my old friend. There's nothing to my statement, just as there's nothing to your statement about a meeting of the minds over a battlefield. That could be taken out of context, as well," Musa said sternly. He waved his best poker face.

He knew the man in front of him had made attempts on his best friend's life, after he had pleaded with him not to. Musa wanted to place his arms around his mentor's neck and snap it. But he had other plans.

"You know, my friend," Papaya said, and continued to walk the track. "We could never be too careful. That's the dilemma we are often faced with, when we take on the task of being a drug dealer on our level. You don't ever have the privilege of trusting someone a hundred percent. But I will tell you this, Musa. I rather be 'dead ass wrong,' than rather be 'dead and right.' I'll take that stance any day of the week," Papaya stated firmly.

Papaya just stood beside Musa and told him that he'd rather be wrong than right. At that minute, Musa knew what needed to be done. "I'm sorry that I took your words offensively," Papaya spoke.

Musa felt that the man next to him was trying to rock him to sleep. "No need to apologize, Papaya. It's nothing but love," Musa replied.

Instantly, Papaya switched subjects. "How is your moms?"

"She's good, just trying to walk these three years down with me," Musa said. He hadn't told Papaya about him getting released in the upcoming months.

"And Ace?" Papaya asked.

Musa hadn't told Papaya about Ace being his sister, and had no plans to do so. "She's trying to hold on. Things are rough, though. They asking for the death penalty."

Papaya stopped in his tracks, for the second time. He stopped in front of the weight pile. Musa looked over Papaya's shoulder and saw his father working curls with a fifteen-pound weight, with his right arm.

"Musa, this is serious. Do you think she would flip to get from under the death penalty?" Papaya asked. The question had Musa mad as fuck.

"Ace would never betray the Mafia," Musa said, with his face balled up.

"No one said she would. But at the same time, Musa, we never can tell what an individual will do when their back's against the wall, especially when their life is at stake," Papaya said, wiping a hand over his slick black hair.

"Point taken, Papaya. But I never like to think of my friends betraying me in such a manner," Musa admitted.

"We never do, Musa, until it's too late," Papaya replied.

"Listen, Papaya, we got an hour before four o'clock count. I'ma head in and get me a quick shower before count. So, I'm gonna check you later."

"Very well then, see you later," Papaya stated, walking off to finish his laps.

Musa made eye contact with his dad, but never acknowledged him. They deemed it was best to maneuver this way. Musa headed back to his unit and hit the shower. He wanted to see Papaya dead. The old man was playing major chess games with Musa. But this was a game he was going to lose. Musa was sure of that.

When Musa got out of the shower, he went straight to his cell and took care of his hygiene. He checked his watch and saw that he had enough time to grab some hot water from the hot water dispenser for a cup of coffee. When he made it back to his cell, the CO was locking his door.

Musa made a strong cup of coffee, black, no sugar, no creamer. He opened his locker and removed a Little Debbie snack cake. Musa wasn't a junk food eater, but under stress, he found comfort in eating junk foot with his coffee. He opened the pack of the oatmeal pie and bit into the pastry. He chased it with a sip of coffee.

"Count time, stand up count!" Musa could hear the CO announce.

He stood to his feet, and moments later, two COs came past his cell and counted him. Musa took another bite of his oatmeal pie before he walked to his cell door to make sure the COs were gone. Before he removed his Galaxy 21 from its hiding spot, he threw the flap up in the window of his cell door. Then he powered up his phone. Instantly, a notification came in. It was a text from his mom, saying she was heading to the storage. He dialed his mother's number.

"Hello," Cheryl answered.

"Hey, mom, you good?" Musa asked.

Cheryl let out a long sigh.

"You know they came for me today, right," Cheryl said with sadness.

"What you talking about, Ma?" Musa took a seat on his bunk.

"This young kid followed me today, from the storage. He had a gun and everything, Musa. I think he had every intention to hurt me."

"What?" Musa said, standing to his feet.

"Some young kid, about 19 years old, tried to kidnap me. He said a guy named Pop-Roc, or some shit like that, sent him to watch me, kidnap me, and bring me back to him," Mama Cheryl was speaking fast.

Musa was ready to die and kill, at the same time. He would kill for his mama, hands down. And dying for her was something he was willing to do every day of the week.

"The kid's name is Pepper, and he said that the guy, Pop-Roc, and Brim are together."

"Hold up, ma. Start from the beginning. Don't leave nothing out," Musa said, needing the full story so he could process it.

When his mother finished conveying the events to him, he was pleased to know his mama wasn't slipping, and she had outsmarted Pepper. He was thankful that Pop-Roc's dumb ass sent a young, unseasoned goon to grab his mother. He was relieved that his mother was safely enroute to Atlanta. But he still didn't feel right, knowing that a man was in his mama's house with a gun. He had to put his plan in motion before Brim or Pop-Roc did something stupid to his mother.

"Ma, stay on the road, and don't stop until you get to your sister's house."

"I wasn't planning on stopping, son. The only time I'm stopping is for gas, food, or to use the bathroom," Mama Cheryl confirmed.

"Okay, that's good. Ma, I'm sorry for placing you in this situation. I love you, Ma. I'm sorry," Musa said.

There was a pause on the phone. All Musa could hear was the Porsche eating the road up.

"Musa, don't be sorry. Fix it. I love you, too," Mama Cheryl stated, before disconnecting the call. Musa could hear that his mother was fighting not to cry on the phone, and that angered him.

He dialed another number, before reseating himself on his bunk. The phone rang four times before it was answered.

"Aye, Shoota, we need to talk."

Chapter 14

"I remember only months ago we tore this very club up. Now we are here, standing as a united front," Brim said, standing at the tip of the strip club Stadium stage. Next to him stood Pop-Roc. Both, Money Mafia and Oxon Hill Mafia Boyz, stood at the base of the stage. Brim had rented the whole club out for this occasion. He bought out the bar, as well as had the owner supply forty strippers for the event.

"We come together as a ban of brothers, one family, one Mafia, with one common goal. And that goal is to grow, expand, and get money. This merge is not for the criminal lifestyle, but to go legit, to even go corporal."

A few members held a bottle in the air, acknowledging Brim's statement.

"The way we make it is to make this a real Mafia family. We must be on the same accordance. I ask Money Mafia to acknowledge Pop-Roc as a leader, as your second in command. Do anyone object to this merge on Money Mafia's behalf?" Brim asked. He stared over the sea of men, waiting for an objection. There was none.

Pop-Roc took the lead. "I once read in the book of *48 Laws of Power*, that If you want a loyal friend, pick a man you once feuded with because you place him in a position to prove his loyalty to you. This merge is a testament to that." Pop-Roc paused for special effects. "Is there anybody from Oxon Hill Mafia that oppose this merge?" Pop-Roc saw a few frowned faces, but for the most part, they were with his decision. Seeing that there were no objections, he looked at Brim and smiled, saying, "Let the merge begin."

Brim removed a long, gold dagger from the small of his back. He wrapped his hand around the blade and Pop-Roc wrap his around the top part of the blade. Brim pulled the blade downward, with one swift motion, putting a small slice in Pop-Roc's and his hand. Blood slowly trickled from both wounds. The two locked bloody hands and sealed the merge by announcing Money Mafia in sync.

The club erupted in cheers.

"Let the party begin. Where the hoes at?' Brim shouted. They must have been on stand-by to get to the money, because as soon as Brim made the statement, the strippers stormed the room.

***

Ace had just come back from a legal visit. She sat on the table, watching the women in her unit. Her lawyer advised her to wait and see if anything unfolded in the case. Ms. Stoner informed Ace that it was too early to start focusing on the death penalty. Her lawyer ensured her that there was a long way to go before they got there. But Ace wasn't a fool. She watched *Law & Order* and *Forensic Files*. Ace knew that they had enough evidence to convict her twenty times over, so she knew it wouldn't be a major task to get her sentenced to death. The thought placed goose bumps up and down her back.

Ace was talking to Tammy last night. They were discussing the death penalty that Ace was facing. Tammy was her girl, but last night, she said some of the dumbest shit ever. Tammy stated, in most cases like hers, the government would let her plead out to a life sentence to avoid the death penalty. Ace knew Tammy didn't mean any harm, but who wants to plead out to life in prison. Ace would rather die than spend the rest of her life in prison.

Mrs. Braxton, the wife of Musa's parole officer, was the only witness, and she was screaming loud and clear. She told about her husband's crooked dealings with shaking the parolees down and blackmailing then to keep their freedom. She even told how her husband targeted Musa. The government had overwhelming evidence against Ace. They had caught Ace with the weapon that killed Mr. Braxton.

Ace shook her head. Then her thoughts went to Brim and her grey eyes turned a shade darker.

Brim was the enemy in the ranks the whole fucking time. Ace's heart rate sped up and her hand went to her chest, where Brim had shot her. If Ace had to slay a whole village to get to Brim, she would. That was how deep her hatred for Brim ran. There was no doubt in her mind that Musa would serve her dish of revenge to Brim. And Ace was content with that.

Ace did a survey of the unit, and what she saw frustrated her a great degree. Ace saw broken women that were trying to find their way out of a bad situation. She wanted to help the women, even though all of them hadn't treated her well when she was first admitted into the unit. The women on her unit were just broken products of their environment.

What could a woman do, when all her life she'd been handed and birthed broken dreams? It was unreal that at a very young age it was planted into the female mind that a man would come and marry her, and make life better, or that loyalty conquers all. Ace was sure most of the women that were in her unit were there behind some type of man, herself included. Most women thought having money was power. That was why they did forbidden things for money. All of it was false dreams.

No one ever told them of the pain and suffering that a man would take them through to become his queen. And once he did decide to marry her, she'd realize that being married wasn't all it was hyped to be, nor what people said it would be. They'd never tell you that loyalty came with sacrifice, and most times, the sacrifice was done for an individual that was not even loyal to you.

Money is power, when you obtain it in the right manner. Making money on your back, just to put food on your stomach, is not power. It's degrading in the highest form. And for a woman to obtain her funds in this form, she must turn off all emotional connection. And if she did that, she'd become less of a woman because women were created to be emotional creatures. This epiphany brought Ace sadness. Tears eased from the corner of her eyes. She wiped them away. Ace closed her eyes and said a quick prayer, asking God for guidance.

Chapter 15

Cynthia sat in her living room, watching The Hustle, starring Jennifer Lopez and Cardi B. She was amazed at how those two chicks could work the pole the way they did. Only if she had the skills to maneuver on a stripper pole, she would take her old ass in the strip club. Body wise, Cynthia could keep up with the young women in the club, but she knew that she lacked the skills and the stamina.

Then Cynthia grew sad. She started second guessing Brim and her relationship. She felt that it was the young women in the strip clubs that were keeping him away from home, and more so, the reason why he still had her living in the LeDroit Park Housing Projects. Brim had this big ass house in Maryland that she had only been to twice. Brim hadn't invited her. She had been loyal to him, since they decided to make it official between them.

Being in a relationship had Cynthia stressed out. And the fact Brim didn't come home to her anymore had her feeling insecure, especially once she found out that he invested in a porn company with Pop-Roc. All the project chicks had been telling her how Pop-Roc had been on camera, fucking the shit out of broads, like it wasn't nothing. Cynthia just knew that Brim was fucking them same dirty ass bitches, because he wasn't coming home laying D on her. She just knew that, sooner or later, there was going to be a video of Brim having sex with some bitch that was way younger than her.

Brim took care of Cynthia but that wasn't enough for her. She wanted a real relationship. She wanted out of LeDroit Projects.

Cynthia let out a sigh. She needed a phat blunt and a stiff drink. She had a bottle of Hennessey Black in the kitchen cabinet but needed some good bud to go with it. One thing about living in the hood, you didn't have to go far to find some weed.

Cynthia paused her movie and got off of her cream-colored leather sofa. She pulled her white booty shorts out of her butt and crease, and went over to the window. She saw the young boys out there blowing weed, but she knew that, most likely, they weren't smoking that grade A. And if they were, she didn't need their broke asses smiling in her face or sniffing around her, just for a blunt or two. Cynthia saw Jus-Blaze getting out of his BMW. She knew that nigga had what she was looking for. So, she opened up her window.

"Heeey, Jus! I need to holla at you. Come up and holla at me, please," Cynthia said, in her ghetto fabulous voice.

Jus-Blaze threw a finger up, telling her to hold on, before he went over to holla at the hustlers that stood in front of the building. Cynthia watched Jus-Blaze intensely. She liked how he moved. His swag was always on point.

"Let me get out this window before I get myself in trouble," Cynthia stated to herself, after feeling herself become moist from watching Jus-Blaze.

Cynthia closed the window and went to the kitchen to retrieve the Henny Black from the cabinet. She grabbed a glass, dropped four ice cubes in it, and poured herself a nice size drink. She took a sip, letting the cool liquid slide down her throat. A knock came to the door and she knew it was Jus-Blaze. She went and opened the door.

"Wassup, Cyn?"

"Ain't shit, I need something to smoke, and I know you got some smoke. So, blow something with me, please. I got a few dollars for you."

"You wild as fuck for that. I will never charge you to smoke with me. We damn near family," Jus-Blaze said, walking in behind Cynthia.

He tried not to look at her ass, but it was too damn phat to not look at. When he got to the living room, he saw the movie on pause.

"Let me find out your ass up here watching Hustle." Jus-Blaze laughed, taking a seat on the sofa and removing an ounce of white widow and some Backwoods from his pocket.

Cynthia came out of the kitchen with the bottle of Hennessey Black and two glasses, one she was already sipping from. She sat the bottle and glass on the table in front of the sofa and took a seat next to Jus-Blaze.

"I heard about the merge, Jus," Cynthia said, catching Jus-Blaze off guard. "I don't think that Brim should have done that, though. But what do I know?" Cynthia said, shrugging her shoulders and taking a sip from her glass.

Jus-Blaze didn't want to speak on the merge. He didn't know if Cynthia was trying to pick him for information for Brim.

"It is what it is, though. All we can do is go with the flow. But why you say you don't think it was a good move?" Jus-Blaze asked, while putting heat to the Backwood he'd just rolled.

"Damn, that shit is gonna have a bitch bent in here," Cynthia said, as soon as she smelled the Blackwood burning. "But I say that just for personal reasons. It was like when Musa was here, I saw more of Brim. But now that he's running things, I don't see him as much. And plus, how can you trust a man after you had past issues with him? That shit doesn't make sense to a bitch, Jus." Cynthia started feeling the Henny take effect.

"That's just how shit be sometimes."

"Brim gonna fuck around and let Pop-Roc kill him. I don't see that shit happening too many times in the hood, Jus-Blaze," Cynthia stated blatantly.

Jus-Blaze didn't know how to reply to Cynthia's statement. He had been plotting the same move. He was planning on killing Brim to make it look like Pop-Roc did it, or vice versa. He just hadn't worked out all the details yet. He wanted to be in position to capitalize off the situation, however it went done.

"Have you heard from Musa or Ace? I wanted to go see them and show them some love," Jus-Blaze said, switching up the subject.

"I haven't heard anything about Musa, except that he has to do three years for that violation. I seen on the news that the State of Maryland is seeking the death penalty for Ace."

"Damn, that's fucked up!" Jus-Blaze couldn't believe them white folks were trying to kill Ace's fine ass.

"Are you gonna pass the Backwood, nigga? A bitch tryna smoke." Cynthia was reaching for the Backwood and trying to take it out of Jus-Blaze's hand. "I don't know about going to see Musa. He would have to place you on a list. But you can go online and setup a video visit with Ace. You can do that with the phone," Cynthia said between puffs.

"Shit, set up a visit for me, then," Jus-Blaze said, unlocking his phone and handing it to Cynthia, who logged on to Maryland's DOC website. She typed in Ace's name.

"What's your name?" Cynthia asked.

"Justin Blaze."

"What? You don't look like a Justin. I thought they just called you Jus-Blaze because you be smoking all the damn time."

"Whatever, and you better not be telling everyone my government name, either. And why you know about Maryland visitations in the DOC?"

"Boy, I've done had a boyfriend or two in every county jail in the DMV," Cynthia stated and started laughing.

"Cynthia, you said that shit like you proud of it," Jus-Blaze said, laughing.

"Okay, you are scheduled for tomorrow at 3:30. It's a 30-minute visit. All you have to do is log on to their site ten minutes before 3:30, and she will be there," Cynthia said, handing Jus-Blaze back his phone.

"Jus-Blaze, let me ask you something?"

"What is it?" Jus-Blaze poured himself a drink.

"Is Brim fucking other bitches?" Cynthia asked.

He could tell that Cynthia was going through something.

"Come on, Jus, you can tell me," Cynthia pressed. She laid a hand on Jus-Blaze's thigh and gave it a squeeze.

He knew if he said yeah, he would be able to fuck Cynthia right there on the sofa, but he wasn't with fucking niggas' women. And if Cynthia wanted to give him some pussy, then he wanted it because she wanted to give it to him, not because she was hurting over some nigga.

"I don't know what Brim is doing, when it comes to that," Jus-Blaze said, moving Cynthia's hands from his thigh and getting to his feet. He dumped about 12 grams of white widow on the table.

"Where you going? You not gonna watch the movie with me?" Cynthia asked.

"Naw, baby girl. I got shit to do. You got some bud. I got to bounce," Jus said, checking Cynthia's thighs out before her left.

Chapter 16

The Next Day: 3:30

"This is some bullshit," Jus Blaze mumbled as he sat in his vehicle and leaned back against the leather seat, with his phone in hand. After logging into the video call ten minutes prior, as Cynthia instructed, he grew restless, waiting for Ace to appear. Ten minutes felt like a lifetime to him. He was an impatient nigga and sitting still was out of the norm for him. Looking over at the clock on his dashboard, the time read 3:30. He was two seconds from logging off when, suddenly, the screen jumped in a strange way, before Ace appeared on the screen.

Damn.

Ace was still beautiful and fine as hell, even with the prison gear she sported.

"Jus? Wha-what?" She started to ask when Just Blaze stopped her.

"What's good ma?"

"Uuhmm."

"I know you surprised to see me, but I had to check on you and made sure you good."

"Uhh, okay," Ace replied, not sure how to take Jus Blaze visiting her, even through video.

He laughed as he studied her facial expression.

Fine as hell.

He always thought she was a beauty and viewing her then, with no fancy hairdo, nor designer clothing, nor jewelry adorning her body, he was in awe. He lusted momentarily, before he remembered the true reason he wanted to speak to her in the first place.

"What's good, ma?" he asked, and once again, he smirked at the leery expression on Ace's face. She was never one to fool easily and he always loved that about her. He then decided, that gaining her cooperation was not going to be easy, so he instantly thought of a different approach.

"Nothing's good, as you can see. So, what's up with you? I know you not checking up with me just to see if I'm good."

"Damn, ma. I can't just check on you?"

Ace's facial expression answered his question, and he just had to laugh again.

"Say less," he said, as he held his hands up in mock surrender. "Well, you look good," he complimented her, attempting to make small talk. But once again, Ace was not having that shit either.

"What do you want, Jus?" she asked in a no-nonsense tone.

He smirked, once more, and shook his head. *This broad is nothing to fuck with.* His thoughts lingered for a second, before he spat out what he knew would get him what he really wanted.

"Damn, ma. I really was checking on you and making sure you good. But I was also trying to catch up with Musa, but I'm not on his visiting list."

"Get in touch with him for what?" Ace wondered in a suspicious tone.

"Damn, ma," he chuckled before he spat out, "Well, I thought he should know that Brim merged Money Mafia and Oxon Hill Boyz.

"What?" Ace was in disbelief, and anger instantly overwhelmed her.

"Yeah, man, shit is real," he let out. He watched as Ace's expression changed to one he'd never quite witnessed before.

"And it's about to get," she stopped mid-sentence, remembering where they were.

"Write this number down, Jus, and finish this conversation by calling that number," she said suddenly, and Jus Blaze understood.

He reached over in his glove compartment and pulled out a small notebook and pen. Ace wasted no time reciting a number to him, which he wrote down.

"Thanks, ma," he said.

Ace simply nodded her head and chucked up the deuces. She was too pissed to say anything else.

Jus Blaze watched as she stood to her feet, and the video ended seconds later.

He instantly dialed the number Ace gave him and prepared for the must needed conversation with Musa.

***

"This nigga watched too many movies."

"Never mind that shit. When did this nigga get a pool table?"

Tuning out the voices of his soldiers, Pop-Roc was in another zone. He stood over his defenseless victim, who was laid partially naked, strapped to a newly purchased pool table, sporting only a pair of Calvin Klein boxers. To say he was upset was an understatement. They were currently occupying an isolated area of the strip club, which was necessary for the task at hand.

"Yo, Pop-Roc, man, I tried," the victim expressed in a muffled tone.

"What, nigga? I can't hear you," he lowered his head towards the victim's ear.

"I tried, mannn."

Pop-Roc looked over towards his soldiers.

"I still can't hear tis nigga."

They smirked, before Pop-Roc turned his attention back to the young victim. He removed a grey duct tape, which was strapped to the victim's mouth.

"Yo, Pop-Roc! I'm sorry! I tried! I didn't mean to let her get away," he screamed, only angering Pop-Roc.

He hated a crying ass nigga. In this life, *take all Ls like a G* was his motto. So, the fact that Pepper was crying like a bitch, instead of taking his punishment like a man, only infuriated him.

"Shut the fuck up, nigga," he yelled. He then grabbed a pool stick, which was laying on the pool table, and slammed it across Pepper's back. The impact was done with so much force, it broke in half. He then grabbed a second pool stick and repeated the gesture.

""Aaah shit," Pepper screamed for mercy, but his screams fell on deaf ears.

Pop-Roc repeated the gesture over and over, resembling the character, God, from the movie *In Too Deep.*

Brim showed no sign of slowing down, as he punished Pepper for allowing Cheryl to get away. There was no fucking up allowed in his organization, and it was a must Pepper understood that, by any means necessary.

Pool stick after pool stick was used to serve as Pepper's punishment, until there were none left.

Chapter 17

Thoughts of his mother invaded his mind. Musa laid back on his bunk, with his hands tucked behind his head. He was envisioning some strong dude, creeping through his mother's apartment with a gun, lurking to cause her some bodily harm. Even though he was grateful that she was able to come out on top of a bad situation, the thought alone of someone singling out his mom for some shit that he was involved in had him vexed.

Brim was in violation. Playing games with his mother was something he would never take lightly. He just needed to keep Brim on the hook until he got free. Then he would be able to deal with his slimy ass.

Musa needed to know what the angle was that Pop-Roc came in at. Because the last time he checked, Pop-Roc and Oxon Hill Mafia Boyz was off limits to Money Mafia. From just what Mama Cheryl had told him, somehow Brim and Pop-Roc were in it together. This made Musa wonder if Pop-Roc and Brim were together from the get-go. Musa closed his eyes and contemplated these things.

The vibration of Musa's phone made him open his eyes. He removed the phone from his pocket and looked at the screen. A number that he didn't recognize displayed on the screen. He was hesitant on answering the call, but that little voice inside of him told him to answer the call.

"Hello," Musa whispered into the phone.

"Wassup, Slim!"

"Who you calling for?" Musa asked, with a no-nonsense tone.

"Musa, this Jus-Blaze, Slim!"

Musa instantly sat up on the bed, hearing that it was one of the good men of the Mafia. But just as quickly, red flags started popping up.

"Blaze, my nigga!" Musa spoke into the phone.

"Man, it's been rough as fuck getting ahold of you. Brim had been playing keep away with you. He don't want nobody communicating with you."

"And why is that?" Musa asked, trying to see if he could pick some information out of Jus-Blaze or decipher if he was on the bullshit with Brim.

"At first, I thought Brim just wanted you to see that he could run Money Mafia by himself, without muthafuckas complaining back to you. But once he merged Money Mafia with them Oxon Hill Mafia suckas, it was clear that he didn't want anyone to report back to you about the takeover and merge," Jus-Blaze yammered through the phone.

"Brim did what?" Musa was mad as fuck. Now the pieces to the puzzle were being fitted in their proper place. Brim and Pop-Roc were the ones, that's what the nigga Pepper had told his mama.

"From your response, this is new to you," Jus-Blaze said.

"The news came across my table, but I just thought it was talk. Blaze, how did you get my number?" Musa asked, changing the subject.

"I got it from Ace. I had a video visit with her today."

Musa's face frowned. He felt a certain way about Jus-Blaze seeing Ace.

"Yeah, Cynthia, from around LeDroit Park, put me on game how to visit her. So, I set up a visit and Ace gave me your number."

Musa was going to have to verify Jus-Blaze's story, but he wanted to push to see if he could trust him. He knew Ace was going to call him tomorrow night.

"Aye, Musa, them niggas Sharkhead and Stink jumped ship. They out here rockin' hard for Brim and his movement," Jus-Blaze stated.

This news had Musa in his feelings. He let them same niggas eat off his plate and they forgot him as soon as he took a loss.

"So, what you going to do about it?" Musa asked.

"What you mean, what you gonna do about it? The question is what you want done about it?" Jus-Blaze replied.

"This life comes with a set of codes. For every violation, there is a penalty. You know what codes that have been violated and you know the penalties."

"Say less, Slim. I'm on it."

"Leave Brim and Pop-Roc for me. I'm gonna hit you in a few weeks. Stay on point out there, and handle that business," Musa said, disconnecting the call. He immediately called Shoota, who answered the phone on the second ring.

"Musa, what's good?"

"A lot, there has been a change of plans."

***

Locating Brim wasn't a hard task. That was normally how it was when niggas were too comfortable, moving through the city. Hell-Cat thought to himself, as he sat on the passenger seat of the black Honda Accord with a 30-round Glock resting on his lap. Bagz was behind the wheel. They had been following Brim off and on for a while now. They almost had his everyday routine. They had worked out the best place to make the hit on Brim. Tonight was the perfect night to bring Brim to his demise.

Hell-Cat sat low in the passenger seat. He took a pull of the Newport that was hanging from the corner of his mouth.

His eyes stayed alert under the fitted he had pulled over them. He was geekin' for the kill. Hell-Cat was a savage in the killing field. Once any nigga got on his radar, it was hard to get him to fall back. But one thing he hated the most was feeling like he was being used. He kind of felt that way with Shoota. He felt that Shoota came to B-More, opened up shop through them, and disappeared.

Fuck if he got shot or not. He felt that Shoota got shot and it scared his ass. Now Bagz and him don't see Shoota anymore. But they were still pushing his work and taking orders from him, like some foot soldiers. And that shit was bothering him. He wanted to express his feelings to Bagz about what he was feeling, but he knew his crime partner was loyal to Shoota.

Before they met Shoota, they were pitching nickel bags of scramble on the east side of Baltimore. Now, with Shoota's product and guidance, they were controlling a few spots in Baltimore.

Shoota stayed true to his word. He sent a team of professional Mexican killers. They came in and eliminated all those that were against their Money Mafia movement. The team was so professional that they made their hits without a trace of them even being there. This made the takeover smooth because this left the remaining crew uncertain of where the hit came from. It also left them still hungry for product, because their supplier was now deceased. So, when Bagz and Hell-Cat came through, they easily accepted the new plug and structure. But with Shoota absent and playing behind the scenes, Hell-Cat was still feeling a certain way. He felt that Shoota should have been in the fields with them.

"Aye, Bagz, what really good with Shoota?" Hell-Cat asked, letting the car window down and releasing the Newport out the window.

Bagz kept his eyes on the back of Brim's truck.

"What you mean?" Bagz replied.

"I'm talking about how this nigga ain't coming around no more. He's just sending contract killers and product, and got us out here doing all the work."

Bagz glanced at Hell-Cat to make sure he was serious, and that cold, hollow look he held in his eyes allowed Bagz to determine he was dead ass serious.

"Yo, you picking the weirdest fucking time to have this discussion. But what you want fool to do, stay on the block with us and pitch dope packs out a basement? Naw, Hell-Cat, can't you see that Shoota is on a totally different level? And hopefully, by fucking with him, one day we can lay back outta sight and call the plays, and continue to get this money. In the last three weeks, we made over a quarter of a million apiece. Niggas not eating like that in our city, but we are, so why worry about if Shoota's here with us or not. Shoota put us in a position to eat like a king. Everything the nigga was gonna do, he did it. So why stress about shit that's not affecting us or stopping us from getting money? Now get your head in the game. He getting ready to park," Bagz said, and nodded his head towards Brim's truck.

Hell-Cat sat up and clutched the Glock. He watched Brim pull up in the parking lot of the apartment complex. Brim hopped out and walked into the apartment building. They parked a few parking spots down and got out.

They knew that Brim didn't spend any more than five minutes at the residence. They didn't know if Brim was picking up work or money. They knew that he came past the apartment before going home at night. He always came out with a bag. So, it had to be either money or drugs.

The move was to wait until Brim came out of the building and got into his truck. Then they would advance from the shadows and do the deed of murder. Those five minutes it took for Brim to come out of the building seemed like forever. Hell-Cat and Bagz were walking with guns drawn. They could see Brim walking out of the building.

Bagz's burner phone vibrated. It was the phone that Shoota called on. He quickly opened the text. Bagz watched Brim stop on the step of the building and place a call on his phone.

Bagz read the text from Shoota: *Stand down, don't move.* Bagz quickly texted back: *We got him in our sights now.*

Shoota replied: *Stand down.*

This shit was frustrating to Bagz and Hell-Cat because they'd spent weeks doing their homework on Brim. They felt defeated when Brim got in his truck and drove away.

Chapter 18

"I'm telling you, Stink, that nigga Jus-Blaze is soft as fuck. I seen his type many times before. I'm telling you, Brim needs to have his wings clipped, because the way he moving is fucked up," Sharkhead complained.

"What proof you got to convict him? He might not like how Brim handled Musa, with the takeover. That's some hoe shit Brim did, by waiting until Musa went to prison to switch up on him. I don't like the shit that he did, and I'm sure that Jus-Blaze's young ass don't like it either. But he's like me, he's on the money train with Brim, and he's not getting off the train for no fuckin' Musa," Stink stated firmly.

"I don't give a fuck what you say, Jus-Blaze can't be trusted. And I'm going to have a talk with Brim about Jus-Blaze."

"Man, you getting ready to get some shit started. Why don't you put a tail on him and see how he's moving before you go do all of that bullshit, accusing the man of some bullshit that might not be true," Stink said, trying to rationalize with Sharkhead.

They'd been sitting in front of Sharkhead's house for the past ten minutes, smoking a blunt together, talking about Jus-Blaze.

"What time you gonna get in traffic tomorrow?" Stink asked, while Sharkhead was inhaling the blunt. He was tired. He was ready to go home to fuck his side bitch, while his baby mom was visiting relatives.

Sharkhead let out a cloud of smoke, looking at the clock on his dashboard. It read 3:15 AM. "I'll probably be leaving the crib around 10 or 11."

"Alright, I'll meet you at Ace Electronics around 12 to grab the work-"

Tap. Tap.

The tapping on the back passenger window made Stink and Sharkhead jump. Jus-Blaze opened the door and got in.

"Look at y'all scared asses. You muthafucker's jumpy as a bitch! Let me hit that, Shark," Jus-Blaze requested the blunt.

"Ain't nobody jumpy, nigga. I wish a nigga would try me. And what the fuck you doing around my house, three something in the morning?" Sharkhead stated with suspicion in his voice. He turned around in the passenger seat to get a good look at Jus-Blaze.

"Man, I couldn't sleep, so I got in my whip and drove around. On nights that I can't sleep, I always drive through where you and Stink live to make sure that everything alright. I'm always checking up on the fam, whether they know it or not." Jus-Blaze let the lie smoothly roll off his tongue.

Stink looked over at Sharkhead with a dumb look in his eyes that said, *See, nigga, the lil homie is straight.*

Sharkhead didn't have a reply to Jus-Blaze's statement, so he passed the blunt to him.

Jus-Blaze took a deep pull of the blunt and closed his eyes. He held the smoke there for a few seconds before he blew out the smoke.

"I heard from the homie Musa," Jus-Blaze said, causing Sharkhead and Stink to cut their eyes at each other.

"Oh, yeah, what he talking about?" Sharkhead asked.

Jus-Blaze took another pull of the blunt. "He said that every violation comes with a penalty," Jus-Blaze said nonchalantly, without a care in the world.

But the statement made the hairs on Sharkhead's and Stink's neck stand up.

"What would make Musa send us a message like that?" Stink asked, feeling very uncomfortable with Jus-Blaze sitting behind him.

"Ain't nobody said Musa sent y'all a message. This nigga Sharkhead asked me what Musa was talking about and I told him. What makes you think he was directing the statement towards you and Sharkhead? And even if he were sending you a message, that shouldn't mean shit to you. The last time I checked, you both just in it for the money," Jus-Blaze said with a smirk on his face. He took another pull of the blunt and closed his eyes.

Sharkhead watched Stink watch Jus-Blaze through his rearview.

"Pssss! Even if Musa was talking sideways out of his neck with that message, I wouldn't give a fuck. I'm my own man, and I do what the fuck I want. And I get money with whoever I choose to get money with. I'm not letting a nigga in jail keep me on a leash and dictate who I get money with, when he's in there and can't even dictate his own life. Man, miss me with that dumb shit," Sharkhead said aggressively.

Jus-Blaze still held his eyes closed. Smoke seeped out of his nose, while he listened to Sharkhead speak from his foul heart.

"I don't think Musa is trying to dictate your movements. I think he just wants those who he broke bread with to have that same loyalty they had in his presence, outside his presence.

"Man, there you go talking about that loyalty shit again. If you want to be loyal to a muthafucka that's in prison, then that's on you. But stop beating my eardrums up with that bullshit," Sharkhead said, turning around in his seat to look at Jus-Blaze.

Jus-Blaze slightly opened his eyes. The weed had his eyelids heavy. He could tell the weed he was smoking was high grade.

Stink fidgeted in his seat. He still felt uneasy with Jus-Blaze sitting in the back of his truck. Jus-Blaze was getting irritated at how Sharkhead was addressing him.

"Aye, Sharkhead, why you always on that ra-rah shit with a nigga?" Jus-Blaze said, hitting the Backwood again.

"Man, this my muthafucking mouth. I say what the fuck I wanna say out of it. And give me my muthafucking smoke back, nigga!" Sharkhead reached in the backseat and snatched the Backwood out of Jus-Blaze's hand. "Fuck you talkin' about, this my muthafucking mouth," Sharkhead mumbled, turning around in his seat and taking a drag from the Backwood.

The gesture angered Jus-Blaze. He took a deep breath.

"Oh, Musa said some other shit, too," Jus-Blaze said through clenched teeth.

"And what's that?" Sharkhead said, annoyed.

"Musa said when a dog that you been feeding bites you, the penalty for that is to put him down," Jus-Blaze said.

He lifted his 9mm Sig with the silencer on the end of its barrel and squeezed the trigger. Sharkhead's head jerked forward and a mist of blood splattered across the windshield and dashboard.

Stink was caught off guard by Sharkhead's brains being blown out over his dashboard. He slightly turned, facing Jus-Blaze's smoking gun, which was pointed at him, and mumbled, "So, it's like that?"

"Yeah, nigga, it's like that," Jus-Blaze said, pulling the trigger, sending Stink into eternal sleep.

Chapter 19

"Aye, Hell-Cat, you been my nigga since we were eighth grad-ers, so I know when something is eating at you. So, spit that shit out so we can chop it up and clear our vision to the bag," Bagz said, breaking some bud down on the black table that rested in front of the sofa he sat on.

The ounce he was breaking down was so potent, it could be smelled across the room, where Hell-Cat sat in the recliner with a Mack 12 across his lap.

Hell-Cat came out of his daze, hesitant to reveal what was bothering him. "I'm just fighting with something, Bagz, but it's not about nothing," Hell-Cat replied, adjusting his body in the recliner.

"What, you over there stressed about, Ma Dukes or your baby moms?" Bagz continued to dig.

The duo had been friends for many years. The two were both the only child from their parents. So automatically, when their friendship became tight, they viewed each other like brothers.

It was a coincidence how they met. They went to the same middle school, but they didn't personally know one another.

There was a Black Asian chick by the name of Lyn, who had recently started attending the middle school. She wasn't giving any of the boys no talk. Well, at least that's what it seemed like, until Hell-Cat and Bagz showed up to her house at the same time. Bagz showed up with a dub bag of weed, and Hell-Cat had a fifth of Henny. Both pursuers had ended up at Lyn's door at the same time. Instead of them falling out, like suckers, they plotted on how to run a train on Lyn.

When Lyn opened the door and found Bagz and Hell-Cat on the other side of it, her heart and her mouth dropped. But before she could respond, Bagz and Hell-Cat kissed Lyn on each cheek, and pushed their way into the apartment, acting like nothing was awkward about the situation.

Lyn recovered from their surprise visit quickly. "I see that my fantasy is about to come true," Lyn said, with a smile on her face, closing the door behind her.

The statement had Bagz and Hell-Cat baffled.

"I want to have sex with the both of you at the same time," Lyn said, biting her bottom lip.

Hell-Cat and Bagz looked at each other and smiled. They blew Lyn's back out. That was their first threesome. And from that day forth, they had been running tough together.

"Ma Dukes good, she enjoying the house I just bought her. And baby moms can't stop driving around Baltimore in the Lex truck. So, everybody good, Bagz," Hell-Cat said, nonchalantly.

"So, what the fuck's going on with you?"

Bagz unwrapped the cherry flavored Backwood and dumped the tobacco inside the ashtray. Then he started to dump weed into the Backwood.

Hell-Cat was still hesitant to address what was on his mind. But he sat on the edge of the recliner seat and spoke.

"To be one hundred with you, Bagz, that shit that Shoota pulled last night, with the hit on Brim, was some fuck shit."

Bagz's facial expression turned to a look of annoyance, and Hell-Cat saw it.

"Hold up, Bagz, let me speak my peace. You asked me what was on my mind, so hear me out. I'm not feeling how shit is transpiring with the nigga. He waited until we did all that footwork on the nigga Brim. We were down to the wire on making the hit, and he hit you, telling you stand down, like we some fuckin' soldiers in a fuckin' army." Hell-Cat was getting agitated, just thinking of the situation. "We were out

100

risking our lives for this dude, Bagz, and he's taking shit for granted."

Bagz said nothing. He lit the Backwood and continued to let Hell-Cat vent. He wanted Hell-Cat to get everything out of his system.

"This nigga been missing in action for a minute. Then he popped back up, moving with all this security, like he the last Don, or some shit. Bagz, I know you gonna think I'm tripping, but I think he had Bump and Money Rage killed."

"What makes you say that?" Bagz asked, speaking for the first time since Hell-Cat started venting.

"You ever paid attention to how Money and Bump just disappeared off the face of the map? No one seen them niggas. You know my baby moms is cool as fuck with Bump's sister. Baby moms said Sandy, Bumps sister, told her the day Bump went missing, he told her that him and Money was gonna go meet the DC connect, and the only person that we know at the time that's outta DC is Shoota." Hell-Cat paused to see if what he was saying was making any sense to Bagz.

Bagz let out a cloud of smoke. "Aye, Hell-Cat, you overlooking details. Shoota already informed us them niggas were stealing, and he had them offed."

"And you believe that goofy shit?" Hell-Cat asked.

"Why not believe it, Hell-Cat? What's the reason Shoota got to lie?"

"He got every reason to lie. That nigga wanted a piece of B-more and you know that Bump and Rage would never just give it up to him. But with them out the way, he easily came in and swooped up a place in B-more, without him really stepping foot inside this city, and without even putting in any work." Hell-Cat pleaded his case.

"What the fuck you mean? That nigga has put some work in. Who fucking hitters have been cleaning up them muthafuckas, who been showing opposition towards this Money Mafia movement? They were Shoota's hittas. We been riding smooth with expanding Money Mafia. Why make a big deal on how he's running shit? I think that you on some geographical shit. The world and the niggas that live in it is bigger than Baltimore. You got to see beyond the streets of B-more and the niggas that roam them. I don't know who really knows the truth behind the death of Money Rage and Bump, but when them niggas was around, they weren't letting us eat like the nigga Shoota. And that's real talk Hell-Cat," Bagz stated taking another pull of the Backwood.

"Yo, ain't nobody on some geographical shit. I'm just saying, if the nigga was a real street general, like he came in confessing to be, then he should show it," Hell-Cat said bitterly. He was offended that Bagz called him out on being geographically set tripping.

Bagz's statement was on point. Hell-Cat didn't like the fact Shoota was from DC and was in B-more making moves that he could only dream about making. But Hell-Cat would never let Bagz know that.

"Come on, fam, we talked about this shit last night. You can't expect Shoota to be out in the field with us, when he's the plug himself. Didn't you say that your Ma Dukes is enjoying the house you just bought her, and that your baby moms is zipping through the city in that pretty ass Lexus truck, huh? Man, it seems like you focusing on all the wrong shit. You need to be focused on how we are gonna stay on Shoota's good side to keep this money rolling in," Bagz said, passing the Backwood to Hell-Cat.

"Because if the wishing well ever dries up, then we are hit because there's no way we could keep up with this city's demand for the dog food," Bagz said, getting up and walking towards the bathroom, leaving Hell-Cat to ponder on his last statement.

The thought of the plug being cut off scared Hell-Cat. He would do anything in his power to keep eating the way he was. And thinking about all the money he had stashed at his mother's house in her basement made him realize that, no matter if a muthafucka from Texas or DC helps you get money, it's all spent the same. And that thought alone made Hell-Cat stop trying to find fault in Shoota's actions and embrace the fact that, without Shoota, him and Bagz would still probably be selling nickels and dimes of scramble. Shoota turned them both into bosses in their own city, so he couldn't do anything but tip his hat to Shoota for that.

Chapter 20

Two Months Later

Moses finished offering two Prostrations in prayer of repentance. He asked Allah to forgive him for his past and present sins. He also asked his creator to bring Musa into the folds of Islam and protect him from any curse of Shaitan. Moses folded his prayer rug up and placed it in the plastic bag with the rest of his property. He grabbed a picture of Cheryl and him, when they were young, and he kissed the picture of Cheryl's beautiful smiling face. He placed the picture in his bag and tied the bag up tightly.

The cancer that was eating at Moses's body had him feeling weak and nauseated, but he forced himself to complete his task.

Moses could feel the cancer in his body, and he knew that his days were numbered on this earth. There was no escaping it. He had stopped accepting treatment for his cancer.

He wiped the light coat of sweat from his forehead and removed the small phone from his pocket. Musa gave him the phone after they determined that it would be best for them not to be seen together on the yard, or anywhere in the prison. Musa gave Moses the phone so they could communicate and so Moses could talk to Cheryl and Ace. Ace and Cheryl didn't have a clue what was going on.

Moses dialed Cheryl's number. She picked up on the second ring, sounding sweeter than Beyonce's vocals.

"Hello," Cheryl answered the phone, but Moses didn't say a word. "Hello," Cheryl stated again.

Moses was taking in Cheryl's voice. He held his eyes closed. "It's me, Cheryl," Moses whispered.

"I know who this is. I see your number on the screen of my phone," Cheryl stated giggly. "Are you okay, Moses? You sounding a little down today?" Cheryl asked.

She knew about his fight with cancer, and she also knew he had refused treatment. Cheryl knew Moses was ready to die, but embracing death is never easy.

"Yeah, I'm wonderful, love. But I need a favor from you."

"Okay, what is it?" Cheryl became more serious and her voice became concerned.

"You remember that Alicia Keys song you always used to sing to me?"

"Oh, my god, Moses, you talking about, *If I Ain't Got You*?"

"That's the one, baby."

"Moses, I forgot all about that song. I haven't sang that song in years, let alone heard it. I don't even know if I remember all the words to the song, Moses."

"Well, just sing what you know, Cheryl, please," Moses pleaded.

Cheryl could sense his sadness, and something came over her that made her feel like this was her last conversation with him. Cheryl cleared her throat and closed her eyes. She started to sing the song from the pit of her stomach.

"Some people live for the fortune. Some people live just for the fame. Some people live for the power. Some people live just to play the game. Some people think the physical things define what's within. And I've been there before, that life's a bore, so full of the superficial. Some people want it all!" Cheryl's voice rose through the phone, and Moses closed his eyes and intensely partook in the sweet melody of her voice.

"I don't want nothing at all, if it ain't you, baby, if I ain't got you, baby. Some people want diamond rings. Some just-want everything, but everything means nothing, if I ain't got you."

Cheryl stopped singing and emotions took over her. Every word touched her soul, like the breath of fresh air invades a baby's lungs for the first time. Tears rolled down her face, and on the other end of the phone, Moses's tears did the same.

"My love," Moses' voice cracked.

"Yes," Cheryl answered in a whisper.

"I love you," Moses said.

"I love you back," Cheryl replied.

"Take care of our son and his half-sister."

Cheryl wasn't mad that Moses had cheated on her with Ace's mom. It was so long ago, it didn't even matter. Plus, she already loved Ace like a daughter.

"I will, Moses. I will," Cheryl cried into the phone.

Moses disconnected the call and sent Musa a text message that he'd typed hours ago. Moses broke the phone up and flushed the remains down the toilet. He then grabbed the ten-inch piece of steel that he grinded down into a sharp point. He tucked the weapon on his hip, exited his cell, and made his way to the chow hall.

***

Musa checked his commissary-bought G-Shock watch. It read 11:23 AM. He slowly moved the cold grits around on his tray. The inmates were chowing down on the prison food that was served to them. But the tray that Musa had in front of him was nothing but a prop, so he could blend in.

Musa was focused on two things: the door to the chow hall and Papaya, who was one table over, politicking with some other major figures that resided in the prison. Musa's palms were sweaty, and he could not bring his heart rate down to save his life. A couple of times, Papaya made eye contact with him, but Musa gave him that dead man stare. You could tell that Musa's stare made Papaya feel uneasy, because he looked across the chow hall towards his two bodyguards. When Papaya met up with the other bosses, it was disrespectful to have the muscle around. So, Papaya was unprotected.

***

Musa shifted his eyes to the door exit, and gave a slight nod. Musa's face broke down into a mug, staring at Papaya, who was busy running his mouth. Papaya did not even notice Musa. But when he did, he stopped talking mid-sentence and nodded his head up, as if to ask Musa what was up.

Musa talked with his fingers. Sign language was something he had learned in prison, as well as 90% of the prison population. Musa spelled Shoota's name out with his fingers.

Papaya's face balled up with anger. Then fear jumped into his eyes, when Musa's father leaned over and whispered in his ear.

"Emma, El Chapo's wife, and Shoota said fuck you!"

Moses removed the ten-inch blade from his waist and slammed it in Papaya's neck. It went in effortlessly. The tip of the shank exited the other side of Papaya's neck. When Moses yanked it out, a mist of blood sprayed the table, and the bosses and shot-callers scattered.

The chow hall went into an uproar. The C.O.'s rushed into the chow hall, while Moses was still stabbing Papaya over and over. Papaya's goons watched in horror. When Moses's knife made contact with Papaya's body, it made a noise like someone was ripping a bed sheet.

"Everyone, get down on the floor!" The C.O.'s yelled as they tackled Moses off Papaya. Moses got down on the floor and laid flat on his stomach. He and Papaya held eye contact. Papaya was five feet away from him. Moses smiled at him and mouthed the words "Money Mafia."

Chapter 21

Musa walked out of Wackin Hunt Prison. The light rain hit his skin and, for some strange reason, the rain felt different on his skin as a free man than it did when he was an incarcerated one. The air that he inhaled in his lungs felt cleaner. He looked back at the prison and a guilty feeling washed over him. He was leaving his dying father behind.

Moses gave the ultimate sacrifice. He killed Papaya so Musa wouldn't be under Shoota's mercy, when he got out. The way Moses figured, he was going to die anyway. So why not go out with a cause? He made Musa promise that he would find a way to get Ace from under the death penalty.

A white Phantom pulled up. Musa had seen the Rolls Royce many times in magazines, but seeing one in person was a different type of experience. The Rolls Royce was breathtaking. The luxury automobile was equivalent to a yacht, but one that had wheels. The Phantom was big and wide, its chrome trimming had it looking like it was only designed for a king.

When the suicide doors opened and Shoota stepped out, the two friends locked eyes and tension crept into the air, until Shoota yelled out, "Money Mafia, all day, every day!" He opened his arms wide.

Musa smiled and embraced his old friend. So many childhood memories of Shoota and him flooded his mind.

"I thought I lost you, Shoota," Musa mumbled in the crook of Shoota's neck. When Musa's mother told him that Shoota was shot and his truck was found abandoned, with Jassii's body in it, he just knew Shoota was dead.

"Shid, I thought I lost you, Musa." Shoota's statement had a different meaning behind it. He was referring to him thinking that Musa had green lighted for Papaya to send them hitta's at him. But Musa had proved that he was his brother's keeper.

"Come on, Musa, let me get you away from this place," Shoota stated, releasing Musa from his embrace.

Musa climbed into the Phantom behind Shoota. The backseat was spacious, and the leather gave the word luxury a whole new meaning. Shoota popped a bottle of Moet and handed it to Musa. Shoota then gave Musa a phone, along with a LV tote bag.

"What's this?" Musa asked.

"Brotherhood," Shoota announced.

Musa unzipped the bag and it was stuffed with bundles of money. Musa looked puzzled.

"That's a meal ticket right there, Slim. Just showing some gratitude for the old man's sacrifice. And I don't mean to offend you. I know that shit was a hard decision to make."

Musa immediately felt bad about his father killing Papaya. He probably would never forgive himself, if he wasn't able to free Ace. He pushed those thoughts to the back of his head and placed the bag between his feet. He took a sip from the bottle of Moet. The champagne bubbles tickled his throat. He watched Shoota twist up the loud pack.

"So, what's the deal with Brim and Pop-Roc?" Musa asked.

Shoota chuckled. "Those bitch niggas running around DC, thinking they running shit. Those muthafuckas don't even have a clue that we are their new plug. We got guns on these clowns at all times, and they buying product from us. You are a fucking genius, Musa. You put this play together, and them niggas fell for the okey doke, like two money-chasing gold diggers." Shoota chuckled again and put some fire to the Backwood.

Musa had Shoota hit Jus-Blaze with two bricks of some pure. Jus-Blaze took the work to Brim with a message to have a sit down to discuss prices with Brim and Pop-Roc, on behalf of a potential new plug. Brim was so pressed to get from under Musa and Papaya that he went and had a sit-down with the new could-be plug.

Once Brim tested the product and saw how the customer responded to it, it was a wrap. He met with Emma, and Brim's stupid ass bit all the way into the bait. Jus-Blaze was playing middleman between Emma and Brim. But the whole time, it was really Shoota supplying the drugs.

"I'm ready to make my move on Brim and Pop-Roc," Musa said.

"What's the rush? Them niggas don't even know you are out, and they don't even know I'm alive. So, we got the chumps in the dark. Let's live a little, Musa. Let's go to Mexico, sit by the pool, and catch some sun. I'm sure that Emma will have a whole train of Spanish bitches there for your enjoyment. I can't participate in the activities because I'm piping down the Mexican Queen Pin."

Musa thought about it for a while before he said fuck it, why not. Then something came across his mind that he had been meaning to ask Shoota about.

"Aye, Shoota, I have some shit to ask you. Why did you tell me not to mention to Ace that you were alive?"

The question made Shoota feel uncomfortable. He looked out the window. He watched as they floated by other cars on the highway.

Shoota was Musa's childhood friend. He knew when Shoota was holding back something.

"Don't sugar coat nothing, Shoota. Give it to me raw, with no chaser," Musa said, watching intensely.

"I was fucking Jassii. Ace found out the night of your birthday party," Shoota mumbled.

"So that's how Jassii ended up in your truck?" Musa asked.

Shoota nodded his head up and down. At the moment, he felt like shit for betraying Ace.

"You know you wrong as fuck, right?" Musa stated.

"I live with the madness daily, and I know what you gonna say. If a muthafucka was backdooring, fucking my peoples behind my back, what would I do?" Shoota retorted.

"Exactly! So now what we going to do about Ace? You can't keep hiding from her."

"Ain't no one hiding from her, Mu. But I like the fact muthafuckas think I'm somewhere taking a dirt nap. It gives me the ability to be invisible."

Musa laughed. "What the fuck you think you are, some immortal thug? Come on, Slim, chill with that bullshit," Musa taunted Shoota.

"You can laugh, Mu, but the facts are that it's hard for a bitch to kill someone that's already considered dead. Twelve already playing around with the idea that I may be dead." Shoota took a swig of champagne.

Musa started to understand more vividly what Shoota meant by being invisible. So, he let the subject go.

It felt good being a free man. The exotic he was smoking on had him feeling good as fuck. He didn't want to get too high, so he gave Shoota the Backwood back. This was the first time he noticed the scar on Shoota's neck, where he must have had surgery to remove the bullet that struck him from Papaya's hittas.

Instantly, his body grew warm from the anger that was brewing inside of him. Papaya's bitch ass tried to take his best friend, his brother, away from him. Musa was glad that he had the privilege of watching Papaya die for his transgression.

"We about to bust the mall down. Then we on the jet to Mexico. We'll spend a few days there, getting you reacquainted with freedom, and some good Mexican pussy. We will put a plan together on how to proceed, dealing with Brim and Pop-Roc," Shoota stated happily. He was happy to have Musa back.

"It's a plan, Slim," Musa agreed, smiling.

"Welcome, Musa," Shoota said, tapping his Moet bottle against the one Musa held in his hand.

Chapter 22

Musa's skin was glistening in the sun. He looked like a rapper, sitting in a lounge chair by the Olympic size pool, shirtless, with a dark pair of Prada shades over his eyes. A diamond Double M chain rested around his neck. Musa nursed a glass of Hennessy Black, while he blew on some exotic bud that was given to him by Shoota.

Musa wasn't even paying attention to the activities that were going on around him. Half-naked Mexican women ran around the pool, water gun fighting. Shoota was on the grill, cooking chicken and burgers. Jus-Blaze was two stepping with a group of women, who wore skimpy thongs and were topless.

Musa's mind was consumed with deep thoughts. He was wondering how his family was doing. He spoke briefly to his mom last night. She was so delighted to hear from him. He promised her that she would see him soon. He needed to hug and touch his mom so badly, but first he wanted to handle business with Brim and Pop-Roc. Mama Cheryl was now out in California, visiting family. She sounded safe and happy, so that brought Musa some relief.

Musa sipped from the glass of Hennessy Black and took a toke of the Backwood. He missed Ace so damn much. He missed her smile, the way she licked her lips, and how her left eye twitched when she was mad or upset. What he missed the most was how Ace felt when she brushed up against him. He hated that Ace was his sister. It made him feel like a creep, when he thought of her in a manner that wasn't appropriate for a brother to think of his sister. He couldn't help it, though. he couldn't turn off what he felt for Ace, no matter how much he tried to convince himself that Ace was that forbidden fruit.

He had set up a video visit with Ace tomorrow. He couldn't wait to see her. Musa's heart dropped when he thought of his father, but he respected his gangster and his sacrifice. A shadow overcast Musa and he pulled out of his thoughts to see who was blocking his sun.

When Musa laid his eyes on the woman that stood over him, he knew that it was none other than Emma. The Mexican Queen Pin was a bad bitch. She stood over Musa with a Versace wrap dress on, that allowed a golden thigh to peek out from its folds. She had perfectly sized breasts that were being held by a bathing suit top. Her flat stomach was flawless, but she had that she-devil vibe reeking off her. When she smiled at Musa, it was like she was trying to seduce him.

"Hola, Mr. Musa," she spoke and extended an impeccably manicured hand to him. "I'm Emma," she stated, when Musa accepted her hand.

The softness of Emma's hand stirred something within Musa. He peeped around Emma and caught Shoota watching them. Musa felt this was a test. Why wouldn't Shoota be here to make the introduction?

"Nice to meet you, Ms. Emma," Musa politely returned her greeting, and let her hand slip from his grasp.

Emma took a seat next to Musa, grabbed the Backwood out of his hand, and took a drag of the blunt. She looked cute as fuck, smoking on the Backwood. Musa peeped her pretty toes and was fighting hard not to compliment her them.

He removed his eyes from her feet and focused them on Jus-Blaze. He was acting a damn fool. He was dancing with a Mexican chick who had on a green thong. He had one of her thick thighs wrapped around his waist and had a mouth full of titty. The group of women had formed a circle around him, dancing and cheering him on.

"Shoota tells me that you want to immediately get back to the action," Emma said in between puffs.

"To get to the money is to get to the action," Musa replied, still watching Jus-Blaze act a fool.

"What it been, seven months, since you seen the action?"

"You say that to say what?" Musa questioned.

He wasn't feeling Emma's vibe. He scanned her lovely home, watching armed guards posted around with fully-loaded weapons. For some reason they became the focus of his attention.

"The business changes so quickly. You blink your eye one second and the business has changed. Why don't you get re-acquainted with the business before you rush back into it?" Emma said with a thick Spanish accent. She handed the Back-wood back to him, after she took one last puff and blew smoke into the air.

Musa accepted the Backwood back and took his own pull from it. Emma looked at Musa and waited patiently for him to reply. Musa blew smoke in the air. He then took a sip from his glass of Henny. He peeped Shoota standing behind the grill, watching them. Musa was stalling with his response because he was trying to get ahold of his anger. He felt some fuckery in the play.

"I don't see why I should prolong getting back to business. If the business changed, I can catch on quick. I'm a fast learner," Musa said, giving Emma a Kool-Aid smile.

Emma smiled back, but Musa could see the fire burning in her eyes.

"You so quick to get down to business, but you haven't handled business with none of the lovely women around you. Maybe being in prison them last seven months has desensitized you." Emma smiled at her own comment.

"A hundred years in prison couldn't do that," Musa replied cockily, but slightly offended.

"Well, enough said," Emma stated. She said something in her native tongue to the group of women that was sitting on the edge of the pool with their legs hanging into the pool.

"Yes, Ms. Emma," a tall beautiful Mexican chick asked humbly. She was accompanied by two other beautiful women.

Musa was confused about how he even missed these ladies. The chick that spoke was so sexy, standing in front of Musa with her light brown double D's encased in her red Dolce & Gabbana bikini top. Her thong bottom was inconsiderably cutting into her lady parts.

Emma said some words in her language. All three women giggled and looked at Musa.

"Hola, Musa!" they all spoke.

Musa tipped his glass in the air, acknowledging the women's presence. All three women were super bad. His manhood started to flinch with desire.

What happened next Musa wasn't ready for. Emma said a few words and all three women pushed their thongs to their ankles and stepped out of them. They turned their backs to Musa, bent over, and grabbed their ankles. Three nicely shaved pussies peeked back at him. Musa heard Shoota let out some laughter.

"Pick which one you would like, Musa," Emma stated.

Musa pulled his Prada shades down on the bridge of his nose and looked over his frames. All three women's kitty cats had a different color tone to them, but all shared a juiciness from the reflection of the sun. Musa could tell whose lady juices were thinner and thicker than the other. But they all had a common denominator. They all made his mouth water and his wood stiffen.

"I want them all," Musa stated, being greedy.

120

No other words needed to be said. The three ladies honored Musa's request, right there, in a lawn chair by the pool. The women stripped him of his pants. All he had on was a pair of Prada shades and his Double M chain. The women had him laid back in the lawn chair, legs spread wide eagle, taking turns swapping his dick in and out of each other's mouths.

Chapter 23

The Next Day

Musa's eyes cracked open. The morning sun was pushing its way through the white linen curtains of Emma's guest room, where he spent his long night. He tried to move, but his body was tangled with the three women he had spent the night with, experiencing the best sex of his adult life.

The night was crazy. The women sexed him like he was some famous rap star, and they were a bunch of groupies. Musa chuckled to himself, just thinking about his crazy night. He didn't even know the three women's names to wake them up to excuse himself. But as quietly and stealthily as he could, he unwrapped himself from them and crawled out of bed.

Musa stood to his feet and fatigue overcame him. His body was sore, like he had been working. For the first time, Musa realized that he still had his Prada shades on. He smirked at the realization, pushed them to the top of his head, and left them there to rest. His bare feet patted against the marble floor.

When Musa first came to Emma's crib, two days ago, he was in awe at her crib. Shoota gave him a grand tour. He knew the chick, Emma, was seeing more paper than Shoota and him had ever seen in their lives. The crib was three stories, seven bedrooms, four full bathrooms, a theater, a game room that was the size of a small rec center, a full gym, and a wine cellar.

When they first pulled up at Emma's crib, there was a Bugatti sitting in the driveway. Musa found the bathroom, stood over the toilet, and drained his bladder. He wobbled on his feet. He didn't know fucking could make you so tired. He knew he needed some protein and some healthy liquids in his body to replenish it.

He thought about Ace and his heart started fucking with him, but he pushed those thoughts behind him. He quickly jumped in the shower, washing the sex off him from last night.

Fifteen minutes later, Musa was heading down to the kitchen. He found the cook there, whipping up breakfast, eggs, toast, and bacon. Musa was an Islamic admirer, so he paused on the pork, and accepted a healthy plate of cheese, eggs, and toast with a glass of water and a cup of orange juice.

He demolished his plate and denied a second serving, when he was asked by the cook. He didn't want to be eating while he was talking to Ace, during the video visit. So, he sipped his orange juice and played around on his phone to pass the twenty minutes he had until he was scheduled to log on to the jail visiting site.

***

Emma gripped Shoota's engorged dick in her small soft hands. Her pinkish nail polish combined with her hand wrapped around his dick looked so sexy to Shoota. Emma inserted Shoota's length down her throat as far as she could get it. Gagging wasn't an option anymore. When she first started sucking Shoota's dick, she used to gag all the time, to the point tears would roll down her face. But now she was a boss giving a boss head. She now sucked and deep throated Shoota's nine inches with perfection. She knew how to get him off by being nice and gentle.

When she first came into contact with Shoota, she had really no intention of fucking him. She was just flaunting her sexiness in front of him, by means of him joining her and her cause. But seeing him shot and nursing him back from the grave, Shoota had lit a flame in her heart. When she would leave to go on business trips, she was so eager to get back home to be around Shoota. But when she fucked around and let Shoota bless her with that big black dick, she was sucking on it like it was a wrap! The little flame Shoota sparked in her heart became a full-fledged forest fire.

Emma ran her hands up and down Shoota's saliva-coated dick in a slow motion. Shoota laid back, enjoying every second of Emma's hot, wet mouth. She twirled her tongue around Shoota's dickhead, glancing up at Shoota. Emma noticed that Shoota's eyes were rolling in the back of his head, when she started teasing his balls with her tongue, while still not missing a beat, as she stroked his dick with her hand. She put Shoota back in her mouth and continued to eat him up.

Minutes later, Shoota's body started to jerk, and a splash of hot semen hit Emma's mouth, causing her to moan, as if it was the best thing she had ever tasted. Emma greedily swallowed every drop Shoota gave her.

Shoota massaged Emma's scalp, while she drained him. She came off Shoota's penis and wiped her mouth with the back of her hand. She crawled up from between Shoota's legs and used Shoota's chest as a pillow. She draped her legs over his. Shoota kissed the crown of her head.

"Your little head skills got way too good," Shoota complimented.

Emma planted a kiss on Shoota's chest. "Everything I do, I'm good at," Emma capped in her thick Mexican accent.

"When you gonna get good at taking dick in the butt?" Shoota asked with a hint of laughter in his question.

Emma's head jerked up from Shoota's chest and she stared into his eyes.

"I will never get good at that, Shoota, because no dick is going in my booty," Emma stated with an attitude.

Shoota burst out in laughter and Emma bit into the flesh of Shoota's stomach.

"Agggh! Chill with that shit, Emma. Damn, I'm just playing," Shoota complained.

Now it was Emma's time to laugh. "That's what you get. I told you about asking me about fucking me in my ass. My asshole is off limits, unless you licking it," Emma said, happily thinking about the thought of her ass being licked.

"Okay, I'm sorry, bae," Shoota said, settling back down in bed.

"When are you going to have that talk with him?" Emma asked.

Shoota let out a deep breath. He wasn't ready to deal with the situation.

"I'm gonna do it soon, Emma. Why you pushing this shit." Shoota became irritated. He hated when Emma became bossy with him.

"Because there's a lot of money Brim and Pop-Roc are making. Why unleash Musa on them and fuck up the money? I'm not saying that Musa should lay down and forget about Brim's betrayal. All I want to do is make sure that, once Musa does make his move on Brim and Pop-Roc, he can handle the workload that comes with removing them out of power."

What Emma was saying was making sense to Shoota, but Shoota knew that Musa wasn't going to accept that shit. Brim burned Musa and shot Ace. There was no way Musa was going to put his revenge on pause.

"I will take everything you are saying under consideration, but I need some time to break the shit down to him in a way that would be acceptable for him."

"Well you need to do that soon because we got Jus-Blaze gearing up to hit them with a shipment. We don't need Musa interfering with the shipment," Emma said, sitting up on the bed.

Her titties bounced under her movement, which Shoota found sexy as hell. He reached over and fingered her long brown nipples. Emma knocked his hand away, and that shit agitated Shoota.

"I will holla at Musa sometime today."

Shoota swung his legs off the edge of the bed and sat up, giving Emma his back. She could instantly feel his attitude, even without him speaking. But she didn't give a fuck about his attitude, all she gave a fuck about was money and securing the whole east coast. Shoota got up and found some sweatpants to put on.

"You want something to drink?" he asked Emma before he walked out of the bedroom.

"No, I'm good," Emma said, climbing out of bed to shower.

Shoota left the room and headed towards the kitchen.

***

"Your daddy sent me a letter, what's that about?" Ace asked, knowing that the only way Moses could have gotten ahold of her address was through Musa.

He hadn't told her about Moses killing Papaya, and as long as she was still sitting in jail, he could never tell her.

"I think you should read the letter, Ace," Musa said.

"I'm not reading shit. Matter of fact, when I get off the visit with you, I'm flushing that shit." Ace pouted.

Musa smiled because she looked so beautiful when she was mad, and the corner of her eye twitched.

"Baby, you wild as fuck. You need to calm your ass down," Musa said.

"So, since you been out, have you gotten some pussy yet?"

Ace's question came out of the blue and caught Musa off guard. He started stuttering.

"I-I-I ain't thinking about no bitch when my Queen is fighting for her life. What the lawyer talking about, though?"

Musa hurried up and changed the focus of the conversation. He felt bad about sexing the three women last night.

"I got a legal visit coming soon. I'm going to sit down with both lawyers, my death penalty and trial lawyer."

"Who you FaceTiming, Mama Cheryl?" Shoota asked, stepping behind Musa, peeping over his shoulder, and catching a glimpse of Ace. He immediately jumped out of view of the camera, but Ace saw him clear as day. Her heart dropped and her anger for him rose.

"I saw your bitch ass, you bitch ass nigga!" Ace yelled.

Musa couldn't do anything but close his eyes and shake his head.

Shoota's face came back in view of the camera. He spoke from behind Musa. "Ace, I'm sorry about that bullshit. I fucked up, Ace. I was tripping, baby girl."

"Man, fuck you, Shoota. And fuck you too, Musa. You out there fucking with that fraud ass nigga. Shoota's a fucking snake. I'm in jail behind your ass, and you out there cooling it with his snake ass. You ain't shit, Musa. You're only loyal to yourself," Ace said, walking away from the screen.

Musa and Shoota sat there looking dumbfounded.

Chapter 24

Ace took long strides back to her cell. She knew the way that she was moving had all eyes on her, but she didn't give a fuck. She had never felt so betrayed in her life. What she was feeling was worse than what she felt that night she discovered that Shoota was fucking Jassii. Ace reached her cell and stepped into it, slamming the door behind her. She was thankful that Tammy wasn't occupying the cell. She needed some time to think.

Ace started pacing the cell floor back and forth. Every few feet she was pounding a close fist into an open palm. Ace was beyond mad. If she was in Musa's presence, she would have tried her best to take his life. She was tired of muthafuckas that were supposed to love her, hurting her the worst. She knew that she never told Musa about how she found out that Shoota was fucking Jassii. Musa must have known about the fuckery. That was the only explanation as to why Musa never told her that Shoota was alive. She and Musa talked many of times. He could have told her that Shoota was alive.

Tears dripped from Ace's eyes. Musa couldn't love her the way that he confessed that he did. Love wouldn't allow you to hurt someone like that. Musa was just like his rotten ass father, they didn't give a fuck about no one but themselves. All the sacrifices she had made for Musa, and that is how he repaid her. She never stole a dime from him, when he went to jail, she stood by his side. She made sure that he had money on his books and phone. She gave him five bricks to start Money Mafia. She even had gotten Brim to kill One Punch to hinder him from testifying against him.

Everything and every sacrifice she made for Musa, she also made for Shoota. But, yet, they both shitted on her, used her like a nut rag. Ace's current situation hit her with the force of an oncoming train. She was facing a death penalty case behind Musa, a man who didn't give a fuck about her. Ace fell to the floor and cried her heart out. She cried because she was so stupid.

A river of tears ran rampantly down her cheeks. Snot drippled in and out of her nose. She cried for all the sacrifices she made for Musa, for all the love she had for him, which he rejected on numerous occasions. It became clear to her that she was just a pawn on Musa's chessboard.

Seeing Musa with Shoota planted a seed of hate in her heart for Musa, and that seed was growing fast. Ace's cell door opened, and Tammy walked in and rushed to Ace's aid. She wrapped her arms around Ace and held her tightly.

"Come on, girl, let it out. Come, baby girl, I'm here for you. Tammy's here for you. She rocked Ace back and forth, and rubbed her back. Tammy's warm embrace was what Ace needed. She felt like everyone in the world had either left her or didn't love her. At the moment, Tammy's embrace made her feel that she was loved, and she mattered.

Ace felt like she belonged in Tammy's arms. She felt so comfortable there. Tammy massaged the soft spots of Ace, and Ace cried harder because it had been so long since she had been touched with such tender care.

Ace maneuvered her body so she could wrap her arms around Tammy. They both were still sitting on the floor. Ace could smell the cocoa butter soap on Tammy's skin, and she loved how it smelled mixing with her natural scent.

"Do you want to talk about it?" Tammy whispered.

"No," Ace mumbled.

Tammy felt how comfortable Ace was in her arms. She felt no other place in the world mattered except for that little place she shared with Ace. She kissed Ace on the ear.

"I'm here for you, Ace," Tammy said.

When she kissed Ace's ear, she could feel Ace lean into her harder. She pressed her head against her lips, signaling to Tammy that she wanted another kiss. And Tammy did just that. She was attracted to Ace, but never thought Ace would ever consider her. Tammy planted kiss after kiss on Ace's ear. "Let me make you feel better, Ace. Let me take your worries away. Let me make you feel good, baby," Tammy said, after each kiss she placed on Ace's ear.

Ace closed her eyes and craved more. After every peck of Tammy's lips, Ace's breath became rigid. She looked at Tammy, and they both searched each other's eyes for confirmation to see if they both wanted to cross that line. Both of their eyes screamed, "Hell yeah!"

The two passionately kissed, and their hands began to roam. They touched each other's breasts and face. Ace was like an ocean between her legs. She was craving a much-needed orgasm.

Tammy was dying to taste Ace. "Stand up," she demanded, and Ace stood to her feet.

She was no longer crying. She had lust and fire in her eyes. Tammy faced Ace and stuck her tongue in Ace's mouth with aggression. Ace welcomed it with her own tongue and aggression.

Tammy worked her hand in Ace's jumpsuit and into her panties. Ace was hot, wet, and ready. Tammy pushed her middle finger into Ace's love box, and it was gushy wet. She worked her finger in and out of Ace, while thumbing her clit. When Tammy removed her hand from Ace's legs, her fingers were soaked. Tammy didn't waste any time tasting the sticky syrup that was on her fingers. She inserted them into her mouth and the taste alone set Tammy's body ablaze.

"Go get naked and get in bed under the covers."

Ace followed Tammy's instructions. She unbuttoned her jumper and let it fall to the floor. She then allowed her white cotton panties to follow.

Tammy's nipples became rock hard, and her mouth watered when she saw Ace's beautiful lady parts. Ace left her white shirt on and climbed in the bed, placing herself under the covers.

Tammy quickly stepped outside the cell and spot checked where the COs were located. They were in the bubble, eating their lunch. Tammy knew she had about thirty minutes before the CO working the floor would make rounds. She quickly eased back into her cell, where Ace was lying in bed, waiting.

Tammy put the window blocker in the cell door's window, so if a passerby walked past, they could not see into her cell. She stripped and gave Ace an eyeful. Ace opened her legs and pushed two fingers into her love box.

Tammy hit the cell lights and immediately got in bed with Ace. Feeling Ace's skin against hers made her pussy boil over with wetness. She lowered herself between Ace's legs and wasted no time finding that little man in the boat. Tammy gently licked and stroked Ace's clit with her tongue.

The way Tammy worked her tongue made Ace think she was part cat, because she'd never before experienced the licking Tammy was putting down on her. Tammy shook her head from side to side, while she flicked her tongue across Ace's clit. She rapidly pushed two fingers in and out of Ace's opening.

Ace's buildup came fast and hard. Her orgasm came like a tsunami. Ace clamped her thighs together, capturing Tammy's head between her thighs. Ace violently shook, trying her best not to scream out in pleasure. Tammy never stopped sucking Ace's clit, until Ace became too sensitive for Tammy to continue. Tammy wiped her mouth.

"See, I knew I could take your troubles away."

***

"Damn, Musa, my bad, Slim, I didn't know you were visiting with Ace," Shoota apologized.

Musa sat at the kitchen island stone-faced. He was trying to find the proper words to address the situation without going in on Shoota. He did not want Ace to find out that Shoota was alive the way she did. Now it looked like he was on some fuck shit. He knew that he should had told her, even after Shoota had asked him not to.

Ace had learned from Mama Cheryl that Shoota was supposed to have been dead. Mama Cheryl had told her right after the police came to Mama Cheryl's house, when they found Shoota's abandoned truck on the side of the road, with Jassii's body inside of it. Traffic cameras caught the assassination attempt.

The authorities knew someone pulled Shoota from his bullet-ridden truck. But they assumed that he was kidnapped and murdered. From the overwhelming amount of blood that was in the truck, they believed that Shoota wouldn't have survived the attack. The authorities did hospital checks and no Shoota popped up, so this strengthened their theory that Shoota was dead.

Musa ran a hand over his face in frustration.

"Fuck, Shoota, this shit wasn't supposed to go down like this," Musa complained.

"I know, Slim, but the shit out there now. Ain't shit we can do about it now," Shoota nonchalantly stated. The anguish he once held in his voice was now gone.

Musa looked at his childhood friend with bitterness in his eyes.

"Shoota, you changed, Slim. You became heartless toward your own people."

"I ain't change, Musa, but Ace don't fuck with me."

"Yeah, you fucked the only person that she ever loved. How the fuck you expect her to feel towards you? You violated, Shoota, not Ace." Musa started to raise his voice.

"And there's nothing I could do to change those facts, but I have been working on some shit that could possibly free Ace," Shoota said, taking a seat across the island from Musa.

"And how the fuck you gonna do that?" Musa asked, like Shoota was on some bullshit.

"Well, I located Mrs. Braxton and her child. That's your ex-parole officer's wife. At any given time, I can make her take a lifelong vacation, her and the child. If Ace has to go to trial, we find the weakest juror, who will take a bribe for two million to cause a mistrial. All we need is one person to cause a mistrial. Three mistrials automatically send you home in the State of Maryland," Shoota said, smiling.

Musa wasn't too happy about the plan Shoota had, but it was better than the plan he had, because he didn't have one.

"Your plan is better than what I came up with at the time," Musa admitted. "I just wish that Ace wouldn't have found out that you were alive the way that she did. She's going to feel like we both betrayed her."

"Man, Ace needs to worry about getting the fuck outta jail, instead of worrying about me beating this dick off in Jassii," Shoota said, with malice in his voice.

He was getting tired of the catering to Ace's feelings. That was the problem. Musa worried too much about Ace's feelings.

"We got other shit to worry about, Musa. Emma wants you to take a back seat on going back into DC. She is with killing Brim, but the fact is, Brim bringing in a truckload of money.

Until we can figure out how you are going to take care of Brim's organization and still bring in the money he's making, you gotta hold off," Shoota said.

"Man, Shoota, you and that bitch on some bullshit. I'm going back into my city to claim my throne, and I'll bring in just as much money as Brim's bringing in," Musa said with conviction.

"How the fuck you so sure about that, Mu? You really think Pop-Roc and them Oxon Hill boys going to get in line behind you and your takeover?"

Musa looked at Shoota as if he had lost his mind. "Shoota, I'm killing Pop-Roc right along with Brim. Kill the heads and the soldiers will fall in line," Musa confessed.

Shoota let out a deep sigh. "Musa, this shit got to be done right. There's too much money involved in this shit to be moving on emotions and feelings," Shoota said.

"Emotions and feelings? Nigga, Brim bit the hand that fed him. He betrayed the Mafia. You talking like that's something small to you. Let me guess, since you fucking the plug, now Money Mafia is too small for you?" Musa yelled.

"Money Mafia never been too small for me. It has always been too big for me. That's why you made Ace your second in command."

"Naw, nigga, that wasn't the reason. Ace made that sacrifice to be Money Mafia's second in command?" Musa said, getting frustrated at Shoota's bullshit.

"What, I didn't make a sacrifice for the sake of Money Mafia? I took a gun charge for your ass, Musa," Shoota said through clenched teeth.

"And Ace killed her stepbrother for the Mafia. How the fuck you think we got our hands on them five bricks?"

This news silenced Shoota. He stared into Musa's eyes to see if he was on some bullshit. But Musa's eyes told him that he was telling the truth.

"Why the fuck you never said anything, Musa?" Shoota asked.

"Because she wanted it to stay between me and her. Ace made me promise her that, no matter what I did with the five bricks, I would always have a place at the table for her," Musa said, pinching the bridge of his nose. This conversation was stressing him the fuck out.

Shoota didn't have words to say about what Musa had just told him. But deep down inside, he felt a certain way that Musa kept this secret from him for so long. This revelation made Shoota realize why Musa treated Ace the way that he did.

"I know your mind is already made up about moving on Brim and Pop-Roc. What can I do to help make the move run sweet, without a hiccup?" Shoota asked.

Musa smiled. Now that was the Shoota he knew.

Chapter 25

Four Months Later

"Brim, Slim, I got some shit that's been nagging at my mental," Pop-Roc said, as he turned down the music that was playing in his Benz. Brim sat on the passenger side.

"What's that?" Brim said, watching the scenery float by him.

"How you really feel about Jus-Blaze being the middleman between us and the plug?"

Brim let out a deep breath. "At this time, Pop-Roc, I don't like it. I think he's taxing us on the prices," Brim mumbled.

"Brim, we got to look deeper into this shit. Sharkhead and Stink get hit. Then Musa just up and cut ties. Then this nigga, Jus-Blaze, comes up with a plug. I think some fishy shit is going on," Pop-Roc confessed.

Now he had Brim's attention. "So you think the nigga, Jus-Blaze, on some fuck shit?"

"I don't know, Brim. But some shit is not right. I can feel it, man. I can feel that shit in my bones."

It had been months since Stink and Sharkhead had been murdered, and there hadn't been anyone linked to their murder. The streets weren't even talking about that shit, and that had Brim nervous for weeks now.

"Do you think that Musa is really the plug, and he is supplying the work through Jus-Blaze?" Brim asked. He was desperately in need of answers.

"I don't know, Brim. The product is way different from the shipments we used to get from Musa and his people. I'm just confused why the plug chose to deal with Jus-Blaze, rather than deal strictly with the individuals that had the money," Pop-Roc stated.

Brim's mind was running. He always knew Musa to be a very calculated type of nigga. Hands down, he was smart. *Could Musa really be pulling strings while he was still in prison? Was this the reason Mama Cheryl just got up and disappeared?* Brim thought to himself, as he scratched his goatee.

"What's your thoughts, Slim?" Pop-Roc asked.

Brim closed his eyes and exhaled deeply. He was frustrated about why things weren't going according to plan. He had the whole DC, Maryland, and Virginia on lock, but yet he didn't have a secure plug. The nigga Jus-Blaze didn't even come around no more. All he did was drop the work off and picked the money up. It was more like he worked for the plug than Money Mafia.

"We put in an order to double the shipment. We tell Jus-Blaze that we are spending too much money with the plug not to meet in person. We let him know it's a must that the plug meet on the next exchange. If the plug doesn't show up, we dome check Jus-Blaze and keep the work and money," Brim said calmly.

***

Musa stood and watched them lower his father into the ground. Mama Cheryl got the call from the prison officials that Moses had died in the hole, due to complications from cancer. It hurt Musa to know that his dad died alone, in a dirty cell, but he was prideful that he had a dad that made the sacrifice that he had for him. He wiped tears from his eyes. Mama Cheryl stood beside her son with her arm wrapped around him and her head leaning on his shoulder. Tears trickled down her face as well.

One of the requests Moses made clear was that he was Muslim and he wanted to be buried as one. When Moses died, Musa had his body flown back to DC, and turned over the Masjid that was located on 18th and Monroe, N.W. Iman Abdul Aziz had Moses taken care of. Once Moses body was delivered to the Masjid, his body was bathed and oiled down in Sandalwood. Then the body was wrapped in white cloths from head to toe.

Once the Muslims started to cover Moses' grave, Musa said a silent prayer and escorted his mother to the car that was waiting. Jus-Blaze and Shoota got in a truck together and followed them out of the cemetery. Musa was going to take his mother to the airport so she could fly back to Atlanta to be with her sister, until he was able to execute his plan, handle Brim and Pop-Roc, and reclaim Money Mafia.

Once Mama Cheryl was secured in the back seat of the Range Rover, Musa got in behind her. The driver pulled out of the Islamic cemetery. Musa's phone started to vibrate. He answered on the second ring.

"Wassup, baby girl?"

"I'm just calling to check up on you. How was the funeral? Are you alright?" Ace asked, her voice laced with concern.

"Yeah, I'm good, baby. Getting ready to head to the airport and drop Mama off."

When Mama Cheryl heard this, she rolled her eyes. She didn't approve of Musa messing around with Ace in that manner. Ever since she found out that Ace was Musa's sister, she had forbidden their relationship.

"Musa, I know that it's too late, but I feel bad that I didn't give him a chance," Ace said and started crying.

"Ace, don't cry, baby. Trust me, though, he loves you. He made a great sacrifice for you. So, hold on to the thought that he went out this world loving you." Musa could hear sniffles on the other end of the phone.

Ace had conned an officer to bring her a phone. And for the last two months, she had been calling Musa daily, helping plot and plan revenge on Brim. She even forgave Shoota, and they had a chance to talk their problems out. Everything was almost normal again. All they had to do was handle Brim and get Ace out of jail, and Money Mafia would be back on top.

"I know, Musa. I just wish that I would have spoken with him," Ace said through tears.

"I know, love, I know," Musa said, letting out a sigh.

"Musa, let me get off this phone. I think the C.O. is about to make rounds," Ace suddenly stated.

"Alright, hit me later. Love you!"

"Love you, too!" Ace said, disconnecting the call.

Musa laid his head back on the headrest and closed his eyes. He had a lot on his plate, and in the next few days, things were going to get real hectic. He just hoped it went as planned.

If this didn't go according to plan, he could very well lose his life and fuck up the relationship Shoota had established with Emma. Since Musa had been home, she had treated Musa well, despite her asking Musa to stall his plans to seek revenge against Brim and Pop-Roc. He honored her request. Now, in the next few days, he would be on go mode. He would have to hit Brim quick and smooth.

"Musa, baby," Mama Cheryl said, breaking Musa's thoughts.

"Yeah, Ma," Musa replied.

"Why do you entertain that foolishness with that girl? That girl is your sister, not your woman. That's some sick shit you doing, and I don't respect it one bit," Mama Cheryl complained.

Musa let out a deep sigh, still holding his eyes closed. Musa and his mother had the type of relationship where they told each other everything. They had been through too much to keep secrets from one another. But he wished that he never told his mother that he was in love with Ace, and he couldn't look at her without seeing a lover in her.

"Ma, come on, don't start. We just buried my dad."

"And that same man that you calling your dad is that same man's daughter you talking about you love. I know your father, Musa. I know he didn't and would never approve of you screwing your sister, his daughter," Mama Cheryl said with pure anger in her voice.

Hearing his mother say those words made Musa feel like the scum of the earth, a borderline pedophile, even though Ace wasn't a child. The whole act of messing with his sister was taboo. But he couldn't deny his feelings for Ace. He could feel his mother's eyeballs burning a hole in the side of his face from her staring at him, waiting for him to reply or feedback about Ace being his father's daughter. Musa opened his eyes.

"I know that my pops didn't approve of my and Ace's relationship, but like I've told him, I just can't turn off what I feel for Ace, like a light switch. And for the record, we never had sex, Ma. Me and Ace never been sexually intimate with each other."

"But you have kissed her, and that's unacceptable on all levels," Mama Cheryl said, nose flaring with anger. She was so upset with Musa over this situation. "So, you need to turn it off, and you need to learn to do it quick, because nothing good comes with messing with your sibling. The only thing that comes from shit like that is pain and hardship," Mama Cheryl stated harshly, turning her back to Musa and staring out the truck's window, leaving Musa to ponder on her words.

Chapter 26

"You really think this nigga gonna show up with the connect?" Pop-Roc said, as he paced the floor.

Brim took aim at the Q-ball with the pool stick before knocking the nine ball into the corner pocket.

"I'm hoping that he does, so we can get this mystery over with. I'm hoping that Jus-Blaze comes connected, because I hate to kill him and miss out on the grade A product he been producing," Brim said, as he started to chalk the tip of his pool stick.

He could hear the rain pour down on the roof of Ace's electronic warehouse. The place brought back memories of him and Musa. Even playing the old pool table, with the double M's stamped in the middle, made Brim think of Shoota, Musa, and Ace.

"Well, I hope the same thing. But, you know, I never been a real big fan of Jus-Blaze. He seemed to not want to take the "L" on that ass whipping he got at the club."

"Some losses are hard to take, when you been winning so long. But Jus-Blaze has learned to live with his loss," Brim stated, re-racking the pool balls.

"I'd feel more comfortable if you would make him a memory," Pop-Roc said, staring at Brim.

"Is that how you really feel?" Brim asked.

"Hell yeah. If everything works out and we can deal directly with the plug, then there would be no need for him?"

"I see that you have it all figured out. But to be honest with you, I was thinking the same thing," Brim confessed.

At that moment, his phone started to vibrate. It was Jus-Blaze texting him that he was pulling up out back now.

"They here," Brim announced, putting down his pool stick and picking up his Mack II. Pop-Roc checked his Glocks.

Two minutes later, Jus-Blaze came walking into the warehouse followed by two Mexicans that were carrying two large duffle bags over their shoulders. Pop-Roc and Brim eyed the three suspiciously. Jus-Blaze and the two men dropped the duffle bags on the pool table.

"What's up, fellas? What's up with the long faces and the weapons?" Jus-Blaze stated, looking at Pop-Roc and Brim.

"Just a little precaution," Brim stated.

"Precaution for what? Business always been straight on my end."

"Yeah, you right, and we trying to keep it that way, too," Pop-Roc yammered. His eyes fixed on the two Mexicans.

"Where the plug at? I know these two muthafuckas a'int it," Brim asked.

"Man, the rain has slowed him down. He's like ten minutes out. He's gonna text me when he gets here. But until he gets here, let's do business," Jus-Blaze said, unzipping the duffle bag. Compressed coke, in the form of bricks, stared back at him.

Brim removed a large bag from under the pool table and placed it on the table. He unzipped the bag that held the money. Stacks and stacks of money were stuffed in the bag.

"We won't be making the exchange until the plug gets here," Brim said.

Jus-Blaze gritted his teeth. "Brim, what the fuck going on here?"

"If the fucking plug don't show up, you don't walk outta here?"

"Man, you trippin'. The plug is coming. Matter of fact, this him right now. Let's go out back and meet him and stop playing these dumb ass games," Jus-Blaze said, getting frustrated. He looked at his phone and pushed it in his back pocket.

"Pop-Roc, watch the two clowns. Come on, Jus-Blaze, let's go."

"Stay with the work," Jus-Blaze told the two Mexicans, who seemed to not have a care in the world. Jus-Blaze started leading Brim to the backdoor.

***

Musa could hear everything that was said through his earpiece. He knew that Pop-Roc and Brim had weapons and that Brim and Jus-Blaze were on their way out. He and Shoota held up the position on opposite sides of the backdoor to Ace's Electronics. When the door swung open, Jus-Blaze stepped out, followed by Brim. Swiftly, he was met with Musa's fo'fifth to the jaw. Musa jammed his gun into his face.

"Drop the tool, nigga, or lose your wig," Musa said through clenched teeth.

Shoota snatched the gun from Brim. When he saw Musa and Shoota, he looked as if he had seen a ghost. Shoota could sense his shock.

"Yeah, it's me in the flesh. Now back your ass into the shop."

Brim couldn't even wrap his head around the fact that Musa and Shoota were standing in front of him. He wondered how Musa got out of jail. Everything that he and Pop-Roc had suspected about Musa being the plug was facts.

Brim backed up through the door he'd just come out of. Musa grabbed him by the back of his neck and led him in at gunpoint. Pop-Roc was shocked to see Brim being led in by Musa. His heart dropped. The two Mexicans drew their weapons and pointed them at Pop-Roc.

Jus-Blaze did something he had been wanting to do for a while. He removed his gun from his hip, took aim, popped a slug into Pop-Roc's chest. Pop-Roc's body fell to the floor, his Glocks falling from his hands and sliding only inches away from him. He fought breathe.

"Chill, Blaze," Musa screamed. "Get me a chair and sit this bitch nigga down," Musa ordered.

One of the Mexicans grabbed a chair and placed it in the middle of the floor. The two Mexicans were Emma's people.

"Chico, Flaco, go watch the door, just in case these bitches want to think they smart and brought some backup," Musa stated, and Emma's men followed Musa's orders.

Shoota forced Brim into the chair. Musa stood in front of him. The two men locked eyes. No words were exchanged. The only noise that could be heard was the rain pounding on the roof and Pop-Roc still fighting to get air into his lungs.

"Why, Brim? Why did you betray me? Why did you betray the Mafia?" Musa asked, genuinely. "Brim, I never knew One-Punch was your dad. But at the end of the day, your dad was on some hoe shit. He was trying to put Shoota and me away."

"My dad was struggling with addiction. You could've handled the situation a different way," Brim said through watery eyes.

The backdoor busted open. "Freeze!" A team of D.E.A. agents rushed in, catching Musa and them off guard, and sending them scrambling.

Shoota and Jus-Blaze opened up on the agents, activating a volley of bullets between them. Brim was caught in the middle, and he paid the deadly price for it. His body took on a slew of bullets that ripped through his flesh and bones, killing him instantly.

Shoota kept popping his Glock, backpedaling. He was trying to make it to the front of the store, but his mission failed when a bullet slammed into his forehead, killing him.

Musa was shot in the shoulder and thigh. He laid there, bleeding out on the floor.

Agents surrounded him, guns still pointed at him. "Mr. Musa Blackwell, you are under arrest," a D.E.A. agent said, before Musa passed out from his gunshot wounds.

Chapter 27

Twenty-Two Months Later

"Mr. Blackwell, get ready. I think the jury has reached a verdict," the United States Court Marshal stated firmly, as he stood in front of the holding cell.

Musa was reluctant to remove himself from the steel bench, where he was seated. He stood, holding his head high, with his shoulders back. He refused to allow anyone to see him weak, in the midst of his storm. Musa straightened his black Tom Ford suit out and made his way to the bars of the holding cell. He placed his hands through them, and the Marshal clamped his wrists together with a pair of handcuffs. The Marshal unlocked the cell and Musa stepped out. There was another Marshal there to help escort Musa to the court to find out his fate.

On the outside, Musa looked well put together. But on the inside, he was a mess. He was heartbroken and distorted. He never would have thought it would be Ace who would betray him. But when she took the stand against him and fingered him as the Money Mafia leader, he knew the cost of love and loyalty was death.

F.B.I. and the D.E.A. came to Ace to help bring Papaya and Musa down. They had the two under investigation, but they never had enough to put a case on them. After Ace became aware that Shoota was alive, and felt that Musa had chosen Shoota over her, she became bitter, and revenge oozed from her heart. Ace allowed the F.B.I. and D.E.A. to listen in on Musa and her phone conversations. Through those conversations alone, there was enough evidence to put Musa away for double life.

During those phone conversations, Musa confessed to having Papaya killed by his father, Moses. Musa spoke about how he was going to regain control of Money Mafia, and how he had Brim buying the drugs from him, even after Papaya was long gone. Through those conversations, the F.B.I. and D.E.A. learned of the plot to assassinate Brim and Pop-Roc, and where the location was going to be. The government didn't have many witnesses, but Ace was their main and star witness.

She took the stand and corroborated every phone conversation that she had with Musa. She even filled in some of the missing blanks for the government. Ace did all of this shit because Shoota had fucked her girlfriend, Jassii, and Musa chose to still be brothers with Shoota. Ace even told the feds that Musa had her kill his parole officer, Mr. Braxton, which was a lie. The government granted Ace immunity for her cooperation. Musa shook his head at the thought of that.

The government was so sure of the case they had against Musa that they offered him a plea of 100 years. If he didn't take the plea, he would go to trial and get life. Musa knew it was over for him, so he went to trial with the two hundred and fifty bricks, and the money that was found at Ace's Electronic raid. It allowed the feds to charge Musa with a super kingpin charge under the United States statute, Title 21, U.S.C. Section 848(b). Under that section, it states a person is making a ten-million yearly gross and the penalty carried a mandatory life sentence, without parole.

Stepping inside the District of Columbia's federal courtroom, Musa turned all emotions off. He was numb to the world. There was no need to scan the court for a supportive face other than his mother's, which was attained by the circumstances. The news of Ace's betrayal had hurt Mama

Cheryl so bad that it caused her to relapse. She was back in the streets, getting high.

The courtroom was silent. Musa stood next to his lawyer. Mr. Manny Kinard, who diligently tried to refute the government charges against Musa, but he knew it was an uphill battle, and he knew the jury had a guilty verdict for his client.

The bailiff came from the back of the judge's chamber, leading the jury to the jury box. None of the jurors looked at Musa or his attorney. Once the last juror took his seat, Judge Wiseburg checked his watch for the time and scribbled some notes on a pad, before he began.

"Foreman of the jury, it's my understanding that the jury as a whole has reached a verdict."

"That's right, Your Honor, we have reached a verdict," a Black woman, who looked every bit of sixty, said firmly.

"Could you please stand, ma'am?" Judge Wiseburg asked.

The foreman stood to her feet.

"How does the jury find Mr. Musa Blackwell on the first count of the indictment under super kingpin, Title 21, U.S.C. Section 848(b)?"

"We find Mr. Blackwell guilty, Your Honor," the foreman stated firmly. This time she stared directly at Musa.

"How do you find the defendant on the second count of the indictment, one count of R.I.C.O.?"

"We find Mr. Blackwell guilty on the second count, Your Honor." The foreman never broke eye contact with Musa.

"And the third count of the indictment of first-degree murder?"

"We find the defendant guilty, Your Honor," the foreman stated, rolling her eyes at Musa. And for the first time throughout the whole trial, Musa hung his head.

His mind drifted back to Wackin Hunt Prison yard, where he had a conversation with Papaya.

"How is Ace?" Papaya asked. Musa hadn't told him about Ace being his sister and he had no plans to do so.

"She's trying to hold on. Things are rough though. They're asking for the death penalty," Musa replied.

"Musa, this is serious. Do you think she would flip to get from under the death penalty?" Papaya asked. The question had Musa mad as fuck.

"Ace would never betray the Mafia!" Musa said, with his face balled up.

"No one said she would. But at the same time, Musa, you could never tell what an individual will do when their back's against the wall, especially when their life is at stake," Papaya said.

"Point taken, Papaya, but I never like to think of my friends betraying me in such a manner," Musa admitted.

"We never do, Musa, until it's too late," Papaya replied.

Musa's thoughts came back to the presence, and when he lifted his head, tears of betrayal rolled down his face.

"We never like to think about those who would betray us until it's too late." Papaya was trying to give him a jewel. But Musa was so deeply rooted with love for Ace, he couldn't see that she was the weakest member of Money Mafia.

Musa could not see and realize Ace's betrayal, until she took the stand, raised her right hand, and swore to tell the truth and nothing but the truth. Musa felt so fucking stupid, he wiped his eyes.

"Life's greatest dangers often come, not from external enemies, but from our supposed colleagues, friends, and family, who pretend to work for the common cause, while scheming to sabotage us." Papaya's words echoed in Musa's head. Even though Papaya was a snake, he was still trying to lace Musa with the tools to identify the cancer within his organization.

But Musa was too blind to take heed to the advice Papaya was trying to give him.

Judge Wiseburg dismissed the jurors, after thanking them for their service. "Is there any motion that needs to be filed at this time?" Judge Wiseburg asked from his bench.

"Yes, Your Honor. I will be filing a notice of appeal on behalf of my client," Musa's lawyer stated.

"Very well, and you have 30 days to file the notice," Judge Wiseburg said.

The prosecutor didn't have any more motions to be filed on the government's behalf. His job was done. Another dangerous Black man was off the streets.

"Well, that will conclude our proceedings for today. I'm setting a sentencing date 60 days from today," Judge Wiseburg announced.

The prosecutor and Musa's lawyer checked their calendars, and both agreed on the set sentencing date. Musa took a deep breath that could be heard through the courtroom. He looked back at his mother, Cheryl. She held tears in her eyes. Musa nodded slightly and Mama Cheryl blew him a kiss. Then she got up and left the courtroom.

Chapter 28

Ace had been waiting for so long for this. Her palms were sweaty as she walked out of the county jail. When the cool breeze hit her skin, her pores opened and welcomed the fresh air. She took a deep breath and took in the freshness of the air. She made a vow that she would never love another man in her life, and she would never sacrifice her life for one.

"Biiiiitch!" Tammy yelled, running across the parking lot towards Ace. The two hugged and shared a loving kiss.

Ace pulled away. "I miss you so much." She smiled at her lover.

"I miss you, too, boo. Now let's get the fuck away from this place. I can't wait to get you home so I can show you what I did to the house. I know I sent you pictures, but it's nothing like seeing in person," Tammy said.

They ran and got into Tammy's Acura truck, and pulled out of the county jail parking lot.

Tammy had been waiting on Ace to get out of jail for the last year. Before Mama Cheryl knew that Ace had turned state's evidence against Musa, Ace had Mama Cheryl give Tammy the keys to her house and all her money. Tammy had been living in the same house that Ace once shared with Jassii. The two became lovers in the county, and when Ace confessed what she was doing to Musa, Tammy didn't judge her.

Tammy drove while she massaged Ace's thigh. Ace opened and closed her legs every time Tammy tried to touch her coochie through the sweats she had on. "I can't wait to get you home, Ace. I got a bunch of toys I want to try on you," Tammy said, squeezing Ace.

"Mmmmm, if you keep squeezing my thigh like that, I'm gonna have you pull over and remind me what that mouth does," Ace capped, while biting down on her tongue.

"No need for all of that, we almost to the crib."

"Well get us there," Ace said seductively.

Briefly, Ace's thoughts turned to Musa. Part of her deal with the government was that she wasn't to be released until she testified against Musa, and he receive a guilty verdict. A part of her felt bad, but then again, the other part of her said fuck him.

Tammy pulled up in Ace's driveway. So many memories flooded Ace's mind. Tammy jumped out and ran around and opened the truck door for Ace.

"Come on, baby, I got a surprise," Tammy said, grabbing Ace's hand.

Ace was amazed at how well Tammy had the living room looking. She wasn't into the dark color furniture, but the black leather living room set was cute.

"Sit here, let me get ready. I want to run your bath water real quick, and put something sexy on for you."

Ace smiled and watched Tammy's juicy ass sway side to side. She closed her eyes and bit down on her bottom lip. Tammy's ass got a little phatter since the last time Ace saw her in person. Tammy was thick enough to make Ace want to lick her ass. Ace giggled to herself because she told herself she would never eat ass. But there she was, sitting in her living room, thinking about performing the dirty deed.

Ace's thoughts fell back to a time when she had her butt licked on, and that shit damn near blew her mind. Then her thoughts faded into who had administrated the booty lickin', and her heart grew dark. Even though it had been a few years since Jassii had died, Ace still hated the woman, as if she was standing right in front of her.

"Fuck you, Jassii," Ace mumbled, and pushed her evil thoughts of Jassii back in the creases of her mind.

She took a deep breath and got to her feet. She kicked her Air Max's off her feet, closed her eyes, and took in the softness of the plush carpet that was underneath her feet. She wiggled her toes.

Ace opened her eyes and walked around her living room. She was admiring the few pictures that Tammy had placed on the wall. Tammy had really made herself very comfortable and Ace was happy that she did. Ace stepped in front of a picture of a smiling Tammy, standing in front of her Acura truck, with all of her curves wrapped in a Chanel wrap dress. Ace wondered who took the picture. More importantly, where the picture was taken and why Tammy didn't tell her, or even send her pictures, when she was in the county. She made a note that she would ask Tammy about the picture. She would be damned if she allowed Tammy to do to her what Jassii did to her.

Ace's eyes fixed on the picture next to the one she was just looking at. The picture she was now looking at was of her, smiling bright, eyes glazed over from intoxication. The picture was a half photo. It didn't show her entire body, but you could see the bottle of D'Usse she held in the air, and the two hundred-thousand-dollar Money Mafia chain she had on. She remembered clearly where she was at when the picture was taken. It was at Musa's birthday party. So many memories flooded her mind, which caused a chain reaction.

Tears came down her face. She took this picture at Musa's birthday party. This was the last day they were together in the flesh. She loved Musa and she hated the fact that she betrayed him, but Musa betrayed her as well. The things she gave and endured for Musa to be happy came with invisible wounds that she didn't even begin to know how to heal.

Ace wiped the snot from her nose. She had to place on Musa's heart the same type of pain he had placed on hers. The only way that Musa could feel the burn of his betrayal was for Ace to betray him and turn state's evidence against Musa. Ace didn't give a shit that Shoota had died, she wished that she could have watched him take his last breath. Ace knew that Shoota didn't make Jassii sleep with him, but Jassii was her woman and Shoota didn't respect that fact. Money Mafia had codes of conduct, and sleeping with a lover of a Money Mafia leader was a breach of the code of conduct. So, Ace had no mercy in her heart for Shoota, because he was the one that caused this whole mess.

A pair of arms wrapped around Ace, slightly startling her. "What you in here doing, baby?" Tammy asked.

"Just looking. Damn!" Ace said, turning around to a topless Tammy, who only had on a pink Victoria's Secret thong and a pair of pink, red bottoms to match. Tammy's nipples were already budded, and the crotch of her thong was wedged between the creases of her vagina.

"You like?" Tammy asked, turning around and starting to make her ass clap.

"Hmmmmm! Yeah, I like it," Ace stated, grabbing a handful of Tammy's backside.

"I got something in the bathroom for you." Tammy led the way, giving Ace an eyeful.

Ace walked into the bathroom behind Tammy and was surprised. The light was dim and there were different types of white and pink candles placed throughout the bathroom. There were two bottles of Moet, sitting on ice, in the bathroom sink. Tammy had rose peddles spread across the floor and in the tub, which was full of water and bubbles. Ace was happy and thankful that Tammy went through all this trouble for her.

Ace kissed Tammy and rubbed her butt. The softness of Tammy's skin had her dripping wet. Tammy helped Ace undress and into the tube. The hot, soapy water opened Ace's pores up. The County's water was always lukewarm.

Tammy popped a bottle and handed it to Ace, who greedily drank from the bottle. Tammy lit some sweat-smelling incenses and a Backwood that she had already pre-rolled for the occasion.

"Alexa, play my playlist," Tammy said, and music started playing.

Flaw & All by Beyonce could be heard. Ace looked over on the toilet cover and saw all types of dildos and vibrators. A thought came to her. *If I'm really a lesbian, then why do I use strap-ons and dildos.* But that thought came to an end when she saw Tammy step out of her thong. Ace's mouth watered when she saw Tammy's pussy completely bald. Tammy eased into the tub with her and made herself comfortable. Tammy sat behind Ace, and Ace was positioned between her legs.

"Oh, God, this feels so good," Ace said, getting comfortable between Tammy's legs. She laid her head back on Tammy's breasts.

"Being with someone that truly loves you always feels good, everything else is extra." Tammy started kissing Ace on the crown of her head and massaging Ace's left breast. "Welcome home, Ace."

"Thanks, bae!" Ace replied, taking another sip of Moet.

The duo passed the Backwood and bottle between them for the next twenty minutes, and in between time, kissing and finger popping each other's pussies. Ace sat the bottle of Moet on the floor on the outside of the tub and faced Tammy. "Baby, I want you to fuck me," Ace seductively said, with her face only inches away from Tammy.

"How you want it?" Tammy asked, standing to her feet and grabbing the strap-on that was located on top of the toilet seat with the rest of the sex toys.

Tammy quickly and skillfully strapped on her penis. Ace stood and placed her hands on the tiles of the wall, giving her back to her lover. Tammy wasted no time finding Ace's opening. She held the tip of the strap-on to Ace's entrance.

"How you want it?" Tammy asked again.

"Nice and steady," Ace replied, anticipating the thrusts to come.

Tammy pushed into Ace and immediately found a nice, steady pace that forced Ace to arch her back and moan out Tammy's name.

"Oh, shit. Yes, baby, yes! Oh, Tammy, you so big, Tammy."

All the moaning went to Tammy's head. Tammy started thrusting harder into Ace. When their bodies collided together, it gave off a loud slapping sound. Tammy watched the seven-inch strap-on shine with Ace's juices. The candlelight gave it an exotic look. Ace was already on her second orgasm when the lights in the bathroom came on, causing both women to jump.

"No. No, don't stop," Mama Cheryl said, holding a black gun with a silencer on it.

Tammy and Ace were frozen like two deer caught in headlights. Fear was written all over their faces. Mama Cheryl giggled.

"Look at you two. Now I know what naked and afraid looks like." Mama Cheryl laughed again.

"Mama Cheryl, what the fuck you doing? How you get into my house?" Ace asked, still not coming off the strap-on yet. She was too afraid to.

"I had keys, remember?" Mama Cheryl said with a smile. "When you had your bitch contact me about your money and house, I knew you were on some bullshit. So, before I turned everything over to her, I made a copy of the keys. And my mother's intuition came true, and it surfaced that you had gotten immunity to testify against my fucking son. I knew you were gonna try to live happily ever after with your bitch, after you buried my only child with a life in prison sentence."

Mama Cheryl's nose ran, and she looked worn and broken, but her eyes still held fire in them. Her addiction could be seen by Ace.

"So, now you gonna kill me, Mama Cheryl?" Ace asked, with tears in her eyes.

Ace never even thought it would be Mama Cheryl, who would come looking for her. She always thought it would be Emma, the Cartel Queen, that Musa had told her so much about.

"Why, Ace, why betray Musa? He loved you. That was your brother!" Mama Cheryl screamed. Her hand shook that held the gun.

"Your brother?" Tammy said with surprise, removing the strap-on from Ace's vagina.

Her sudden movement made Mama Cheryl pull the trigger. Phuff-phuff! The gun spit, sending two bullets to the back of Tammy's head. She fell back out of the tub.

Ace started to scream.

"Shut the fuck up!" Mama Cheryl screamed.

Ace forced herself to be quiet. She held her hands over her mouth.

"I have a message for you, from my son. He said you broke the code of silence and, even though you escaped the death penalty once, Money Mafia you won't escape. He hereby sentences you to death."

Before Ace could respond, Mama Cheryl squeezed the trigger of her gun, killing Ace.

Mama Cheryl stepped out on Ace's porch and took a deep breath. She was ready to start her new life.

A black GMC pulled up in front of Ace's house. Mama Cheryl walked to the truck and got in. Once she got comfortable, the question was asked, "Did you take care of business?"

"Yeah, Emma, it's done," Mama Cheryl mumbled.

"Good job, Cheryl. Now let's get you to rehab so we can start your recovery and new life," Emma said, giving her driver the nod to drive off. Mama Cheryl closed her eyes and laid her head back on the truck's headrest.

Epilogue

For the first time in her life, Emma was at a stalemate of what she should do. Over the last few years, certain chains of events had changed her perspective about life, loyalty, and love.

She never intended to love Shoota. Heck, she hadn't realized she loved him, until she learned that he was murdered in the FBI and DEA raid. When Shoota died, the burn of emptiness that she felt in her cold heart allowed her to understand that she was more than a Cartel boss. On the other side of the coin, she was a woman that was capable of experiencing love, who also needed love and affection through this crazy business she had fought so hard to be a key figure in. Emma had to be real with herself. If she allowed herself to openly love, then she would become vulnerable and open to be attacked from all sides, because the business she was in was dominated by men. And the way that men are wired makes them think the female species is weak, when their hearts are clouded with love.

Emma sat in the backseat of her navy-blue GMC, reflecting on her thoughts, while watching Bagz and Hell-Cat politicking on the east side of Baltimore. Since Shoota had been gone and their source of product was cut off, Hell-Cat and Bagz had lost much of the territory that Shoota had them take over. But they still occupied the territories that were bringing in most of the money. Due to the lack of good constant product, they weren't able to maintain their hold of the city.

It had been almost three years since the death of Shoota and the fall of Money Mafia, and Bagz and Hell-Cat were still maintaining. Emma liked that. She was there to introduce them to a new level of the drug trade, which they'd never experienced, but she was hesitant. She wasn't sure if Bagz and

Hell-Cat would conform to her being the food of their growth, or even worse, betray her and place her behind bars.

Emma was a strong, powerful woman, but prison terrified her. The scare with Musa talking recklessly on the phone about her to Ace was a very close call. Even though the Feds or DEA didn't know who she was, the situation made them know she existed, and they wanted to know who she was. Emma was still wanted for questioning about her connections to Money Mafia. But she was not willing to just walk in and be questioned by the FBI or DEA. So, until they found her, she didn't have any plans on talking to them any time soon.

Even though Musa was reckless with her name over the phone, he stood solid on Emma's name when the Feds came lurking and asking questions. A plan was hatched between them for Ace's betrayal, but Mama Cheryl already had a plan of her own. She wanted to be the one to kill Ace for sending her son to prison. Musa had asked Emma to take care of his mother, and she promised she would. Once Mama Cheryl got released from the rehab center, she would be there to pick her up and shower her with love.

Emma could see the potential bosses in Bagz and Hell-Cat, and at that moment, she decided that she would pick up Bagz and Hell-Cat up, treat them to brunch, and discuss their futures and prices.

"Victor, I have seen enough, pull up," Emma ordered her driver and personal bodyguard.

Before Victor could pull the big GMC up to the corner store, where Bagz and Hell-Cat were standing, talking to a group of individuals. A black van pulled up. Two shooters jumped out and sprayed the group. Bagz was hit first. Before he could react, he was already dead from two shots to his head. Hell-Cat caught a bullet in his back, and he fell to the ground.

Emma knew they were the intended targets, because the shooters stood over them both and emptied bullets into their bodies. The shooters jumped back into the van and drove down the avenue for a quick escape. The shooting happened so quickly that it was done in the blink of an eye. Emma shook her head slightly at Bagz's and Hell-Cat's slain bodies as she rode past in her GMC.

She placed her Chanel shades on her face and mumbled, "A minute too soon, and a second too late."

THE END

Lock Down Publications and Ca$h Presents assisted publishing packages.

BASIC PACKAGE $499
Editing
Cover Design
Formatting

UPGRADED PACKAGE $800
Typing
Editing
Cover Design
Formatting

ADVANCE PACKAGE $1,200
Typing
Editing
Cover Design
Formatting
Copyright registration
Proofreading
Upload book to Amazon

LDP SUPREME PACKAGE $1,500
Typing
Editing
Cover Design
Formatting
Copyright registration
Proofreading
Set up Amazon account
Upload book to Amazon

Advertise on LDP Amazon and Facebook page

***Other services available upon request. Additional charges may apply
Lock Down Publications
P.O. Box 944
Stockbridge, GA 30281-9998
Phone # 470 303-9761

Submission Guideline

Submit the first three chapters of your completed manuscript to ldpsubmissions@gmail.com, subject line: Your book's title. The manuscript must be in a .doc file and sent as an attachment. Document should be in Times New Roman, double spaced and in size 12 font. Also, provide your synopsis and full contact information. If sending multiple submissions, they must each be in a separate email.

Have a story but no way to send it electronically? You can still submit to LDP/Ca$h Presents. Send in the first three chapters, written or typed, of your completed manuscript to:

LDP: Submissions Dept
Po Box 944
Stockbridge, Ga 30281

DO NOT send original manuscript. Must be a duplicate.

Provide your synopsis and a cover letter containing your full contact information.

Thanks for considering LDP and Ca$h Presents.

NEW RELEASES

A GANGSTA'S KARMA 3 by FLAME

BORN IN THE GRAVE 2 by SELF MADE TAY

THE BRICK MAN 5 by KING RIO

BABY I'M WINTERTIME COLD 2 by MEESHA

MONEY MAFIA 2 by JIBRIL WILLIAMS

Coming Soon from Lock Down Publications/Ca$h Presents
BLOOD OF A BOSS **VI**
SHADOWS OF THE GAME II
TRAP BASTARD II
By **Askari**
LOYAL TO THE GAME **IV**
By **T.J. & Jelissa**
TRUE SAVAGE **VIII**
MIDNIGHT CARTEL IV
DOPE BOY MAGIC IV
CITY OF KINGZ III
NIGHTMARE ON SILENT AVE II
THE PLUG OF LIL MEXICO II
CLASSIC CITY II
By **Chris Green**
BLAST FOR ME **III**
A SAVAGE DOPEBOY III
CUTTHROAT MAFIA III
DUFFLE BAG CARTEL VII
HEARTLESS GOON VI
By **Ghost**
A HUSTLER'S DECEIT III
KILL ZONE II
BAE BELONGS TO ME III
TIL DEATH II
By **Aryanna**
KING OF THE TRAP III

By **T.J. Edwards**

GORILLAZ IN THE BAY V

3X KRAZY III

STRAIGHT BEAST MODE III

De'Kari

KINGPIN KILLAZ IV

STREET KINGS III

PAID IN BLOOD III

CARTEL KILLAZ IV

DOPE GODS III

Hood Rich

SINS OF A HUSTLA II

ASAD

YAYO V

Bred In The Game 2

S. Allen

THE STREETS WILL TALK II

By Yolanda Moore

SON OF A DOPE FIEND III

HEAVEN GOT A GHETTO II

SKI MASK MONEY II

By Renta

LOYALTY AIN'T PROMISED III

By Keith Williams

I'M NOTHING WITHOUT HIS LOVE II

SINS OF A THUG II

TO THE THUG I LOVED BEFORE II

IN A HUSTLER I TRUST II

By Monet Dragun

QUIET MONEY IV

EXTENDED CLIP III

THUG LIFE IV

By **Trai'Quan**

THE STREETS MADE ME IV

By **Larry D. Wright**

IF YOU CROSS ME ONCE II

ANGEL V

By **Anthony Fields**

THE STREETS WILL NEVER CLOSE IV

By K'ajji

HARD AND RUTHLESS III

KILLA KOUNTY IV

By Khufu

MONEY GAME III

By Smoove Dolla

JACK BOYS VS DOPE BOYS IV

A GANGSTA'S QUR'AN V

COKE GIRLZ II

COKE BOYS II

LIFE OF A SAVAGE V

CHI'RAQ GANGSTAS V

By Romell Tukes

MURDA WAS THE CASE III

Elijah R. Freeman

THE STREETS NEVER LET GO III

By Robert Baptiste

AN UNFORESEEN LOVE IV

BABY, I'M WINTERTIME COLD III

By **Meesha**

QUEEN OF THE ZOO III

By **Black Migo**

VICIOUS LOYALTY III

By Kingpen

A GANGSTA'S PAIN III

By J-Blunt

CONFESSIONS OF A JACKBOY III

By Nicholas Lock

GRIMEY WAYS III

By Ray Vinci

KING KILLA II

By Vincent "Vitto" Holloway

BETRAYAL OF A THUG III

By Fre$h

THE MURDER QUEENS III

By Michael Gallon

THE BIRTH OF A GANGSTER III

By Delmont Player

TREAL LOVE II

By Le'Monica Jackson

FOR THE LOVE OF BLOOD III

By Jamel Mitchell

RAN OFF ON DA PLUG II

By Paper Boi Rari

HOOD CONSIGLIERE III

By Keese

PRETTY GIRLS DO NASTY THINGS II

By Nicole Goosby

PROTÉGÉ OF A LEGEND II

By Corey Robinson

IT'S JUST ME AND YOU II

By Ah'Million

BORN IN THE GRAVE III

By Self Made Tay

FOREVER GANGSTA III

By Adrian Dulan

GORILLAZ IN THE TRENCHES II

By SayNoMore

THE COCAINE PRINCESS VI

By King Rio

CRIME BOSS II

Playa Ray

LOYALTY IS EVERYTHING II

Molotti

HERE TODAY GONE TOMORROW II

By Fly Rock

<u>Available Now</u>

RESTRAINING ORDER **I & II**
By **CA$H & Coffee**
LOVE KNOWS NO BOUNDARIES **I II & III**
By **Coffee**
RAISED AS A GOON I, II, III & IV
BRED BY THE SLUMS I, II, III
BLAST FOR ME I & II
ROTTEN TO THE CORE I II III
A BRONX TALE I, II, III
DUFFLE BAG CARTEL I II III IV V VI
HEARTLESS GOON I II III IV V
A SAVAGE DOPEBOY I II
DRUG LORDS I II III
CUTTHROAT MAFIA I II
KING OF THE TRENCHES
By **Ghost**
LAY IT DOWN **I & II**
LAST OF A DYING BREED I II
BLOOD STAINS OF A SHOTTA I & II III
By **Jamaica**
LOYAL TO THE GAME I II III
LIFE OF SIN I, II III
By **TJ & Jelissa**

BLOODY COMMAS I & II

SKI MASK CARTEL I II & III

KING OF NEW YORK I II,III IV V

RISE TO POWER I II III

COKE KINGS I II III IV V

BORN HEARTLESS I II III IV

KING OF THE TRAP I II

By **T.J. Edwards**

IF LOVING HIM IS WRONG…I & II

LOVE ME EVEN WHEN IT HURTS I II III

By **Jelissa**

WHEN THE STREETS CLAP BACK I & II III

THE HEART OF A SAVAGE I II III IV

MONEY MAFIA I II

LOYAL TO THE SOIL I II III

By **Jibril Williams**

A DISTINGUISHED THUG STOLE MY HEART I II & III

LOVE SHOULDN'T HURT I II III IV

RENEGADE BOYS I II III IV

PAID IN KARMA I II III

SAVAGE STORMS I II III

AN UNFORESEEN LOVE I II III

BABY, I'M WINTERTIME COLD I II

By **Meesha**

A GANGSTER'S CODE I &, II III

A GANGSTER'S SYN I II III

THE SAVAGE LIFE I II III

CHAINED TO THE STREETS I II III

BLOOD ON THE MONEY I II III

A GANGSTA'S PAIN I II

By J-Blunt

PUSH IT TO THE LIMIT

By **Bre' Hayes**

BLOOD OF A BOSS **I, II, III, IV, V**

SHADOWS OF THE GAME

TRAP BASTARD

By **Askari**

THE STREETS BLEED MURDER **I, II & III**

THE HEART OF A GANGSTA I II& III

By **Jerry Jackson**

CUM FOR ME I II III IV V VI VII VIII

An **LDP Erotica Collaboration**

BRIDE OF A HUSTLA **I II & II**

THE FETTI GIRLS **I, II& III**

CORRUPTED BY A GANGSTA I, II III, IV

BLINDED BY HIS LOVE

THE PRICE YOU PAY FOR LOVE I, II ,III

DOPE GIRL MAGIC I II III

By **Destiny Skai**

WHEN A GOOD GIRL GOES BAD

By **Adrienne**

THE COST OF LOYALTY I II III

By Kweli

A GANGSTER'S REVENGE **I II III & IV**

THE BOSS MAN'S DAUGHTERS I II III IV V

A SAVAGE LOVE **I & II**

BAE BELONGS TO ME I II

A HUSTLER'S DECEIT I, II, III

WHAT BAD BITCHES DO I, II, III

SOUL OF A MONSTER I II III

KILL ZONE

A DOPE BOY'S QUEEN I II III

TIL DEATH

By **Aryanna**

A KINGPIN'S AMBITON

A KINGPIN'S AMBITION **II**

I MURDER FOR THE DOUGH

By **Ambitious**

TRUE SAVAGE I II III IV V VI VII

DOPE BOY MAGIC I, II, III

MIDNIGHT CARTEL I II III

CITY OF KINGZ I II

NIGHTMARE ON SILENT AVE

THE PLUG OF LIL MEXICO II

CLASSIC CITY

By **Chris Green**

A DOPEBOY'S PRAYER

By **Eddie "Wolf" Lee**

THE KING CARTEL **I, II & III**

By **Frank Gresham**

THESE NIGGAS AIN'T LOYAL **I, II & III**

By **Nikki Tee**

GANGSTA SHYT **I II &III**

By **CATO**

THE ULTIMATE BETRAYAL

By **Phoenix**

BOSS'N UP **I , II & III**

By **Royal Nicole**

I LOVE YOU TO DEATH

By **Destiny J**

I RIDE FOR MY HITTA

I STILL RIDE FOR MY HITTA

By **Misty Holt**

LOVE & CHASIN' PAPER

By **Qay Crockett**

TO DIE IN VAIN

SINS OF A HUSTLA

By **ASAD**

BROOKLYN HUSTLAZ

By **Boogsy Morina**

BROOKLYN ON LOCK I & II

By **Sonovia**

GANGSTA CITY

By **Teddy Duke**

A DRUG KING AND HIS DIAMOND I & II III

A DOPEMAN'S RICHES

HER MAN, MINE'S TOO I, II

CASH MONEY HO'S

THE WIFEY I USED TO BE I II
PRETTY GIRLS DO NASTY THINGS
By Nicole Goosby
TRAPHOUSE KING **I II & III**
KINGPIN KILLAZ I II III
STREET KINGS I II
PAID IN BLOOD **I II**
CARTEL KILLAZ I II III
DOPE GODS I II
By **Hood Rich**
LIPSTICK KILLAH **I, II, III**
CRIME OF PASSION I II & III
FRIEND OR FOE I II III
By **Mimi**
STEADY MOBBN' **I, II, III**
THE STREETS STAINED MY SOUL I II III
By **Marcellus Allen**
WHO SHOT YA **I, II, III**
SON OF A DOPE FIEND I II
HEAVEN GOT A GHETTO
SKI MASK MONEY
Renta
GORILLAZ IN THE BAY **I II III IV**
TEARS OF A GANGSTA I II
3X KRAZY I II
STRAIGHT BEAST MODE I II
DE'KARI

TRIGGADALE I II III

MURDAROBER WAS THE CASE I II

Elijah R. Freeman

GOD BLESS THE TRAPPERS I, II, III

THESE SCANDALOUS STREETS I, II, III

FEAR MY GANGSTA I, II, III IV, V

THESE STREETS DON'T LOVE NOBODY I, II

BURY ME A G I, II, III, IV, V

A GANGSTA'S EMPIRE I, II, III, IV

THE DOPEMAN'S BODYGAURD I II

THE REALEST KILLAZ I II III

THE LAST OF THE OGS I II III

Tranay Adams

THE STREETS ARE CALLING

Duquie Wilson

MARRIED TO A BOSS I II III

By Destiny Skai & Chris Green

KINGZ OF THE GAME I II III IV V VI

CRIME BOSS

Playa Ray

SLAUGHTER GANG I II III

RUTHLESS HEART I II III

By Willie Slaughter

FUK SHYT

By Blakk Diamond

DON'T F#CK WITH MY HEART I II

By Linnea

ADDICTED TO THE DRAMA I II III

IN THE ARM OF HIS BOSS II

By Jamila

YAYO I II III IV

A SHOOTER'S AMBITION I II

BRED IN THE GAME

By S. Allen

TRAP GOD I II III

RICH $AVAGE I II III

MONEY IN THE GRAVE I II III

By Martell Troublesome Bolden

FOREVER GANGSTA I II

GLOCKS ON SATIN SHEETS I II

By Adrian Dulan

TOE TAGZ I II III IV

LEVELS TO THIS SHYT I II

IT'S JUST ME AND YOU

By Ah'Million

KINGPIN DREAMS I II III

RAN OFF ON DA PLUG

By Paper Boi Rari

CONFESSIONS OF A GANGSTA I II III IV

CONFESSIONS OF A JACKBOY I II

By Nicholas Lock

I'M NOTHING WITHOUT HIS LOVE

SINS OF A THUG

TO THE THUG I LOVED BEFORE

A GANGSTA SAVED XMAS

IN A HUSTLER I TRUST

By Monet Dragun

CAUGHT UP IN THE LIFE I II III

THE STREETS NEVER LET GO I II

By Robert Baptiste

NEW TO THE GAME I II III

MONEY, MURDER & MEMORIES I II III

By **Malik D. Rice**

LIFE OF A SAVAGE I II III IV

A GANGSTA'S QUR'AN I II III IV

MURDA SEASON I II III

GANGLAND CARTEL I II III

CHI'RAQ GANGSTAS I II III IV

KILLERS ON ELM STREET I II III

JACK BOYZ N DA BRONX I II III

A DOPEBOY'S DREAM I II III

JACK BOYS VS DOPE BOYS I II III

COKE GIRLZ

COKE BOYS

By Romell Tukes

LOYALTY AIN'T PROMISED I II

By Keith Williams

QUIET MONEY I II III

THUG LIFE I II III

EXTENDED CLIP I II

A GANGSTA'S PARADISE

By **Trai'Quan**

THE STREETS MADE ME I II III

By **Larry D. Wright**

THE ULTIMATE SACRIFICE I, II, III, IV, V, VI

KHADIFI

IF YOU CROSS ME ONCE

ANGEL I II III IV

IN THE BLINK OF AN EYE

By **Anthony Fields**

THE LIFE OF A HOOD STAR

By Ca$h & Rashia Wilson

THE STREETS WILL NEVER CLOSE I II III

By K'ajji

CREAM I II III

THE STREETS WILL TALK

By Yolanda Moore

NIGHTMARES OF A HUSTLA I II III

By King Dream

CONCRETE KILLA I II III

VICIOUS LOYALTY I II

By Kingpen

HARD AND RUTHLESS I II

MOB TOWN 251

THE BILLIONAIRE BENTLEYS I II III

By Von Diesel

GHOST MOB

Stilloan Robinson

MOB TIES I II III IV V VI

SOUL OF A HUSTLER, HEART OF A KILLER

GORILLAZ IN THE TRENCHES

By SayNoMore

BODYMORE MURDERLAND I II III

THE BIRTH OF A GANGSTER I II

By Delmont Player

FOR THE LOVE OF A BOSS

By C. D. Blue

MOBBED UP I II III IV

THE BRICK MAN I II III IV V

THE COCAINE PRINCESS I II III IV V

By King Rio

KILLA KOUNTY I II III IV

By Khufu

MONEY GAME I II

By Smoove Dolla

A GANGSTA'S KARMA I II III

By FLAME

KING OF THE TRENCHES I II III

by **GHOST & TRANAY ADAMS**

QUEEN OF THE ZOO I II

By **Black Migo**

GRIMEY WAYS I II

By Ray Vinci

XMAS WITH AN ATL SHOOTER

By Ca$h & Destiny Skai

KING KILLA

By Vincent "Vitto" Holloway

BETRAYAL OF A THUG I II

By Fre$h

THE MURDER QUEENS I II

By Michael Gallon

TREAL LOVE

By Le'Monica Jackson

FOR THE LOVE OF BLOOD I II

By Jamel Mitchell

HOOD CONSIGLIERE I II

By Keese

PROTÉGÉ OF A LEGEND

By Corey Robinson

BORN IN THE GRAVE I II

By Self Made Tay

MOAN IN MY MOUTH

By XTASY

TORN BETWEEN A GANGSTER AND A GENTLEMAN

By J-BLUNT & Miss Kim

LOYALTY IS EVERYTHING

Molotti

HERE TODAY GONE TOMORROW

By Fly Rock

BOOKS BY LDP'S CEO, CA$H

TRUST IN NO MAN

TRUST IN NO MAN 2

TRUST IN NO MAN 3

BONDED BY BLOOD

SHORTY GOT A THUG

THUGS CRY

THUGS CRY 2

THUGS CRY 3

TRUST NO BITCH

TRUST NO BITCH 2

TRUST NO BITCH 3

TIL MY CASKET DROPS

RESTRAINING ORDER

RESTRAINING ORDER 2

IN LOVE WITH A CONVICT

LIFE OF A HOOD STAR

XMAS WITH AN ATL SHOOTER

www.ingramcontent.com/pod-product-compliance
Lightning Source LLC
Chambersburg PA
CBHW071210260626
47162CB00004B/1246